CROSSING YESTERDAY

CROSSING YESTERDAY

Women of the Ozarks

THE SCRAPBOOK SERIES BOOK 2

NATALIE R. VICE

CONTENTS

Women of the Ozarks
The Scrapbook Series

Memories of Tomorrow, A Prequel
Tomorrow's Promise
Crossing Yesterday
Unraveling
The Other Side
Wait For Me...

Discover more at
www.facebook.com/NatalierVice
www.natalievice.com

FOR ALL THE "PRIME time" women who are a part of my life. There are too many to name individually; for that, I am thankful and blessed. This one's for you.

Sometimes life gives us magic, something that cannot be explained or reasoned, something or someone that changes the course of our life; call it luck, call it fate, or call it love. Families and true friends bring us magic moments that we collect and remember forever.

- Unknown

CHAPTER 1

"Like a restless leaf in the autumn breeze,
Once I was a tumbleweed.
Somebody tell me please, was I right or wrong?"
Lynryd Skynyrd

AS THEY SPED ALONG the steep and curvy road, the mountains framed either side. The breathtaking view distracted both women.

A gorgeous green canopy topped each towering trunk as it rose from the Ozark soil. The majesty of their height and power left each woman in awe. Sunshine glinted and shimmered on everything it greeted, including the jeep as it hummed its way along the mountain road. The view was a fantastic and inspiring sight to behold. Jo sighed. She had been too long in revisiting her beautiful mountains. As for Gina, she always felt admiration every time she made the trip. As each woman gazed in wonder, the sparse conversation focused on their weekend plans.

"You're gonna love these cabins up here, Jo. None of this was here when we were kids. So much has changed. Max and Maxine moved up here and built a store, an RV park, and twenty cabins. You could say they started their own small town."

"Max and Maxine who? You've not told me their last name."

"Oh, Maximillus and Maxine Durand. They're hilarious and I

can't wait for you to meet them. Both of them are originally from Convent, Louisiana, and got to be in their seventies, although you won't notice their age when you meet them. They cook BBQ (or at least they try), run a small store, and still have time for their passion: the mountains. If my memory is right, they have around twenty folks that stay up here throughout the year."

"Durand? That's George's last name, and he's from Louisiana, too. He's mentioned his parents in conversation; I believe he said they lived somewhere in Missouri, and from what I understand they're a couple of renegades. Anti-establishment, anti-government, really anti- *anything* that's happening with government today." She laughed.

"They said George works in a 'den of iniquity, liars, and thieves'. I wonder if he knows them." There was an unmistakable grin of mischief on her face.

"That describes Max and Maxine. When we stop, I'll let them tell you their story. Everyone here has a story…" she smiled and laughed. "Max and Maxine have a great story! Oh, one more thing, don't ask them about the greenhouse in the back of the store. Not yet anyway."

Jo gave Gina a puzzled look. She opened her mouth to speak as Gina froze in place. She made a gurgled, gasping sound; as though she sucked in enough air to blow up a balloon.

Engrossed in their conversation and view of the mountain, they hadn't noticed the large, black bulky object in the middle of the road. Not until the moment the object stood to survey the approaching jeep.

"Oh, my"… Gina started and then her voice shrank to a whisper. "It's a bear!"

"A bear?!?" Jo shrieked, slamming on brakes and sending them jolting forward. "What do we do now? Get out and ask him if he needs a ride?"

Gina giggled. It was a hilarious vision she of Jo approaching the bear and beginning a conversation.

Uproarious laughter followed the giggle. Along with the memory of her first meeting with "Bear", Polk Ridge's resident "pet" years ago.

"Jo, how many times have we seen bears? This isn't something new… you know bears live in these mountains. Just do what we've always done."

"Really Gina, *really*? What we've always done won't work this time, do you see another way around, *anywhere*?" Mr. Clancy's words echoed in her mind, "*There's always more than one way to skin a cat.*"

Both women surveyed the surrounding woods, searching in vain for an opening that even remotely resembled a road, or trail. Something to give them a way around the still very interested and approaching black bear. As they gazed around, not one inch of the beautiful forest yielded opportunity: not a road, not a trail, not even a path.

"There's nothing, nothing. Not even a decent hole to dart into with a jeep."

"Well, we better hurry; He's decided he'd like to get to know us better, anyway, and gettin' closer by the minute, Jo."

Jo shifted gears, trying to reverse their course. At that instant, the wind swept up the road from behind the jeep providing the bear with a big helping of Jo and Gina scent.

Another car came into view from the opposite direction.

The bear, deciding that there was simply too much activity and human attention focused on his presence, stood once more on his back legs. He was either surveying the odds, or the wind had provided a smell that held more promise than the approaching cars. At any rate, he chose the Ozark woods over the passenger vehicles.

As he lumbered off, Jo and Gina let go a deep sigh of relief. The openness of the Jeep did not afford the protection that their counterparts had in a traditional vehicle. Neither woman wanted to think about what "might" have happened. They were just thankful the bear decided against getting up close and personal.

Gina finally found her voice. "Too bad we didn't have any of those doughnuts we used to get in town. I bet he would've appreciated a taste of something sweet."

Once again, roles reversed, as a shaken Jo interjected, "I'm not gonna get close enough to feed a wild bear a doughnut, Gina. No dice. Not me."

"I remember a day when the sight of a bear didn't upset Jo Felsenthal. You've truly been away too long!"

"You're right about one thing, I have been away long enough to forget the adrenaline rush of meeting a bear. Cyberhackers can be dangerous, but they're not up close and personal, nor do they want to take a bite out of you if they 'hack' you."

"Ok, now that my breathing is returning to normal, how far until we get to the store? I could use something to drink, and a reprieve from the wild beauty of nature. A store and people would fit quite nicely into my plans at this point."

"It's only a few more miles up the mountain. Why don't we skip the hiking this morning, visit with Max and Maxine, and then go hiking this afternoon? Maybe all the bears are finished wandering, and we won't cross paths with one on Lost Valley Trail."

Gina laughed again as she replayed the earlier few minutes in her mind. This would be an interesting weekend.

The women spent the next twenty minutes in comfortable conversation on a much safer topic: Maureen.

"Jo, did you check on your mom before we left? I meant to ask you that long before we got this far into the mountains, but it slipped my mind."

"Yeah, I called her last night before I went to bed. I wanted to make sure she knew we'd be gone and to make sure Stella was coming today to check on her. I think she'll be fine and I'll call her when we get home tomorrow."

"Is her bum leg making it hard on her?"

"Not like I thought, and she is doin'g better with the housekeeping. I'm telling you, I didn't realize how close she might be to depression, until I got there the day after she broke her leg. It was a shock. The house was a mess. I'm still in disbelief."

"Well, as I said, I didn't notice the house when I finally got there the day I found her. I was too concerned with gettin' her to a hospital. I didn't give the house a second look."

"Well, you'll never know how much I appreciate you looking in on her. I should have been home years ago. Instead, I waited on an accident to decide what I should do."

"Look, Jo, if you're not around them on a day-to-day basis, it's hard to realize when your parents begin to slip. You aren't there to notice when they get depressed, or when they have signs of dementia or Alzheimers. It takes daily interaction to recognize those issues."

"I can see that now – I just didn't a few months ago."

"You gotta turn left in a half a mile and then it's only five more to the store. It's 10 o'clock, they should have lunch and sweet tea ready. I should tell you more about Max and Maxine before we get there. They can be quite a handful if you're not prepared."

"No, I can't take anymore 'input' right now. Let's just get to the store, take a break and eat lunch. Then we'll hike and talk. Max and Maxine can't be that much different than any other older couples in the world."

Gina simply smiled. She would let Jo discover the answer to that when she met them.

The curving, winding, barely paved road suddenly straightened, and there was the store. It was such a quaint, long-forgotten country setting, that Jo's eyes widened in amazement.

"It's almost as if we've stepped back in time. I never dreamed this existed here."

The store sat off to their right and looked as if it were built at the turn of the 20th century. Max and Maxine had made sure their store-slash-home was befitting a mountain setting. Old, hand-hewn boards covered the building and porch that wrapped around the front and right side. A stone chimney occupied most of the left side of the building and carefully disguised an area built for smoking and barbecuing. So close were the two structures, you couldn't tell if the smoke curling from the side of the building came from the chimney or the smoker.

Old Coca-Cola signs, Texaco signs, old and discarded automobile tags, and wooden hand-carved signs covered the front of the building. There was an old gas pump at the front of the building, but it was obvious to Jo that it hadn't worked in years. She surmised that it was added purely for aesthetics. Except for the gas pump, the blinking "ATM" sign, and the "We're Open" sign that hung at the front, it could have been an old mountain home. It looked completely untouched by the passage of time; nothing about the building lent you to believe it should be a fixture of 2012. Yet, here it was. And judging from the number of people that occupied the picnic tables on the front porch, it was very much a part of current daily activity.

"Wow, I don't know what I was expecting, but this wasn't it. This place is so cute, it looks as though it's been here for years."

"Yeah, they built it that way on purpose. They've been here ten years or so, but it looks as though it's been here forever. Let's go grab something to eat and let me introduce you."

As the two women extricated themselves from the Jeep, Jo looked around at the rest of her surroundings. The store was on her right, and to her immediate left an entire field of cabins. There were at least ten of them in different shapes and sizes. On past the cabins, Jo could see a drive marked with a sign that read "Cabins 11-20". The drive disappeared into the shadowy folds of the mountain. She saw no evidence of RV's.

"I thought you said there was an RV park? I see the cabins, but not any RV's."

"Oh, they're here, you just have to look for them. When they put this place together, they wanted it to blend with nature. They put the RV's behind the store. There's a small gravel road on the other side of the store that leads to the RV Park surrounded by trees. Max says that way you only have tenants that you want to have. It's filled up over the years by word of mouth. Max invited a few of his friends in the beginning; then they told a couple of their friends. Now, you have a bunch of old hippies and renegades that live here. And according to Max that's exactly the way he wants it."

As they talked, they reached the front porch, and Gina stopped short as she opened the door.

"Ready? This will be so much fun to watch."

She turned to give her friend an innocent look. Jo once again returned her look with a puzzled gaze, but before she could respond, there was a shout from within the store.

"Gina! My goodness, c'mon in here! It's so good to see you."

Maxine stood behind the counter and appeared to be operating the register that sat perched atop. The checkout area was separated from the rest of the store by wooden swinging partial doors. In her haste to get to Gina, Maxine bolted through those swinging doors, nearly knocking them from their hinges.

Jo turned to find the source of the shout. Unprepared for the site that met her eyes.

Maxine Durand was less than 5 feet in height, and just as slender as Gina. Her personality made up for what she lacked in stature. Ebony hair was everywhere. It looked to Jo as if the effort to hold it in the twisted bun (she was sure that was the original intent) had completely failed; possibly because Maxine darted and moved as if someone had lit a fire underneath her. She certainly didn't fit Jo's idea of seventy-ish. Green eyes, weathered skin, and an easy smile completed the small person throwing her arms around Gina.

"Oh, honey, I'm so glad to see you. We haven't talked in weeks and I've got so much news for you."

It was at that moment she stopped, turning her gaze to Jo.

"Is this her? Is this Miss Jo that you've talked about so much?" She turned to look at Jo, waiting for confirmation from either woman.

"Yes, Maxine, meet Major Jorja Felsenthal."

Jo cringed. She had meant to tell Gina just to skip that part. She really didn't want to answer a bunch of questions surrounding her military service. These people might have a negative opinion of a country and government she had served faithfully for so many years.

"Well, *Major* (Maxine emphasized the word) Jorja Felsenthal, I'm very pleased to meet you. You sure hold a special place in Gina's life, and anybody that special to Gina is someone I'm glad to meet.

"Please just call me Jo, Max. I so rarely hear Jorja, I forget who that once was."

"Well, Jo, I hope you like our little community up here. Gina always stays in Cabin 2 when she comes, and we have the best visits. Are you two gonna stay the night tonight?"

Before Jo could answer, Gina responded, "Yes, we are; is Cabin 2 empty? If not, we could stay in another. After all, I didn't call to let you know we were coming. Where's Max? I want Jo to meet Max, too."

"Oh, he's out back taking the ribs off the smoker. Give him just a minute, I'm sure he'll be out to see you. Are you girls hungry? Let me get Lucy to take your order, I need to get back on that register.

I'll have him come out here when he's back in the store. Have a seat honey. Lucy'll be right on out."

Maxine turned, and in just as hurried a motion as she had approached, she left. Leaving Jo feeling as though she had stood in the midst of a whirlwind.

"Well, I don't believe I've ever seen anyone as spry at seventy as Maxine, that's for sure. I pictured her as gray, slow, and not quite so... mmm... boisterous."

Gina laughed. "I told you…"

As she was finishing her comments, a woman that looked to be close to their age approached the table. Jo eyed her and assumed this must be Lucy.

"Hey, Gina. Well, you finally got your friend to come back to her mountains." She smiled at Jo, with a smile that reached all the way to her eyes. Blonde and at least as tall as Jo, she wasn't as overwhelming as Maxine had been. She extended a worn and rough hand towards Jo.

"Pleased to meet you. I'm Lucy, I live and work here. I hope you have a great time visiting us this weekend, and hopefully, these mountains have called you home to stay."

"Nice to meet you too, Lucy. I'm Jo, and I'm sure I'll have a great visit. I haven't visited these mountains in years, and I'm looking forward to hiking the trails I explored as a kid."

Lucy then turned her attention to their lunch order, and once finished, disappeared to the back of the store.

"She lives here? At the store, or here in the mountains?" Jo asked, as Lucy walked away.

"She lives in the RV Park and they trade out her lot rent for her work in the store. I think Lucy's been here almost as long as Max and Maxine. She knew them in Louisiana, and when they came up here, she followed."

"I'll take you over to the RV Park when we've finished eating and introduce you to the folks that stay and work here. There are four that stay year-round, and others that just come for the spring and summer."

In a few minutes, Lucy returned with their drinks and word that their lunch would be ready shortly. Max was in the kitchen, and she told him it was Gina's order he was preparing.

"Max said to tell you he'll be out in a minute to see you and meet Jo. He's never met a 'major' before, so he wants to talk to Jo."

"Oh, no. He'll have a hundred questions, Jo. Might as well get ready. He won't rest until he's quizzed you and shared his opinion of 'government intrusion into his life'; you have to take Max in small doses. At least until you get to know him."

"Great. This should be an unbelievable exercise in restraint."

Gina giggled. "Well, restraint might not fully describe it."

As she finished her sentence, Max appeared from the kitchen, and made his way to their table. Jo gaped in astonishment. If Maxine had been a surprise, Max was a complete shock. George flickered through her mind; she really *was* going to have to ask him if he knew these people.

Maximillus Durand approached the table with the grandeur of a French chef, right along with the apparel that Jo remembered from her days in France. Short and stocky, with fiery black eyes, and a mustache just as black. It was obvious Max reveled in his role as "chef" for the establishment. He wore the traditional chef's attire, replete with a "toque" or chef's tall hat, white jacket and checkered pants. For every quick step that Maxine had made, Max's were just as slow and deliberate.

"Ladies," he slowly released from his lips, as he approached. "Your lunch is served." And he just as slowly, he placed their order on the table. He turned to smile at Jo.

"I am honored to make your acquaintance Major Felsenthal. I

trust you will find our food is excellent, and our conversation even more so. Will you be staying with Gina in Cabin 2 this weekend? I hope I have more time to visit with you later tonight when we have our usual Saturday night campfire."

Before Jo could respond, he turned to Gina. "We've missed you. I'm glad you connected with your friend and you've come to spend the weekend with us."

Jo was still trying to recover from the shock of such a strange little man in such a place as the Ozark Mountains. So much so that it was Gina who answered Max's questions.

"Sure, Max, we're coming to the campfire tonight, and yes, Jo and I will stay in Cabin 2, if it's empty. I want to take her to meet everyone in the 'Park', then we're going hiking on the Lost Valley Trail. We should be back long before the Saturday night gathering."

"Good, I'll talk with you later tonight, then Miss Jo. You ladies please enjoy your lunch, I must return to the kitchen." And with that, Max just as deliberately strode away.

Gina turned to look at Jo, who was still showing obvious signs of shock. She burst into laughter as she surveyed her friend's astonished look.

"I told you they were different."

"You weren't kidding – different is putting it mildly. How the hell did they ever find these mountains and decide they wanted to live *here*? They both look like they oughta be in Hollywood, not here. Not the Ozark version of Dollywood."

Gina continued to chuckle. "Just wait til you hear their story. I'm not gonna ruin it now, you'll just have to wait til tonight. I'll explain 'campfire night' while we're hiking the Lost Valley Trail. You should get a kick out of this event."

Before Jo could ask, Gina stuffed her fries into her mouth. She threw her hands in the air beside her; motioning as if to say "what? I can't talk right now."

Jo sighed. This might prove to be more than she anticipated, and the longed for "rest and relaxation" was becoming a vanishing prospect as each moment passed…

CHAPTER 2

Twenty years now
Where'd they go?
Twenty years
I don't know
Sit and I wonder sometimes
Where they've gone…..

Bob Seger

AS THEY ATE THEIR lunch, Gina explained how the community functioned, especially during the spring and summer months.

"Max and Maxine came up here with a dream of establishing a 'retreat' for themselves and others who wanted a simpler way to live once they retired. They didn't realize, in the beginning it would require so much work. Well, I think Maxine knew, it was just Max that didn't understand."

"Maxine's family has owned several retail stores in Louisiana; in fact, Maxine spent most of her life working in sales. Max, on the other hand, only saw operations from the outside. He is an engineer by trade and retired from an industrial company in Louisiana."

"So, when they came up here, it wasn't long before Max decided he just might need help. The idea for the RV park was born, and several of the residents of the park trade work for a place to stay. It's a win-win for all of them. Max and Maxine have the help they need, and the 'helpers' have a place to stay."

"Well, that's an interesting way to retire, and one I didn't even realize might exist. How did they find them?"

"Most of them are friends they made while living in Louisiana; they both have had a chance to meet so many people in their work they were bound to find a similar souls along the way."

"But you know, there are organizations that do nothing but match people like Max and Maxine, business owners, with retired individuals looking for part-time work. It work's best in tourist places. I researched the options when I got ready to retire, just in case I wanted to travel on the cheap someday."

"Well, I guess you and Melvin could buy a camper and travel around, working *and* vacationing. God knows, Melvin has experience in food service; that's something tourism always needs."

"Yeah, I guess we could, if you could ever get Melvin to talk about retiring. That's not high on his priority list right now."

Something in the tone of Gina's answer gave Jo pause. *It's possible things weren't so concrete with Gina and Melvin. Um... a later conversation.*

As they left the store, Gina led Jo towards the gravel road that would take them to the RV Park.

"You don't wanna drive the jeep?" Jo asked.

"Naw, it's only just a few hundred yards up the road, no need to drive it, it won't take but a few minutes to walk."

As they walked, Jo reached in her pocket to retrieve a cigarette; Gina's groan signaled her immediate disapproval.

"You *still* smoke?"

"Yes, I still smoke. It's one of the few things I've enjoyed for most of my life, and I have no intention of giving up something I enjoy.

Yes, I know what it's doin'g to my lungs, and yes, I know you're like an outcast in society today, but I really don't care. I like it."

"Well, by all means, light'er up!" and Gina began to laugh. "We all have things we enjoy that might or might not be so 'socially' acceptable. Far be it from me to judge!"

Jo could tell her friend had no sarcastic intent. She was poised to ask what it was that she enjoyed that might not be socially acceptable, when the road widened several feet. The trees stopped and gave way to a small clearing.

Jo was once again astonished at the sight that lay before her. Roughly an acre in size, the small clearing was filled with campers, vehicles, and people. It looked as if the circus had come to town. Her eyes took in colorful awnings, grills of all shapes and sizes, and patios inlaid with stones or made of concrete. Yard decorations and lights hung on awnings and between campers. Splashes of color and campers covered the 'Park'.

Activity was everywhere. It was, after all, Saturday and weekend grilling, camping, and gatherings were in full swing.

"It's as if you enter a different world at the park. Let me take you around and introduce you to the folks that are here all year. Thanks to Max and Maxine, I've made some wonderful friends here."

"Ok, you met Lucy at the store. That's her camper right over here to the left; she stays in Lot #1."

It was obvious to Jo that Lucy was a different individual. She had an old Airstream. Silver, of course, and in seemingly great shape, Lucy had added her own individuality to the trailer. On the side of the trailer, someone had airbrushed *"The Silver Bullet – No Seger, No Band"* in bold black lettering. There was no awning in sight, and a lone grill adorned the concrete patio beside the camper. She had, however, installed a small, steel carport beside the camper. The carport sported the same silver color as the camper. Functionality with no frills.

Gina continued to talk as Jo soaked in the area known as "Lot #1".

"Lucy used to work construction, I'm pretty certain she doesn't care much for frills when it comes to 'the comforts of home'. From what I understand, she's more concerned with the function and productivity of her house, not how it looks."

"I see, but I gotta say, she's got one great old camper. You don't see these much anymore, and especially not in such great condition. At least she takes care of it."

"Yes, she does. She's a stickler for keeping her house in order and she works much the same way. I've noticed she does more to run that store in an orderly way, than Max and Maxine. Max says she's 'anal' in her view of work, and he should know, he is a true engineer!"

Jo smiled at Gina. She was familiar with the term, having heard it from George on many occasions.

"Well, she and I have one thing in common. George has used that term to describe yours truly more than once."

"Ok, now on to Lot #2, Bob." As if by telepathic summons, Bob appeared at the door of his camper. Tall and slender, Bob was exactly what you'd expect in the Ozark Mountains. There was gray in his beard, gray in his hair, and wisdom in his brown eyes. Eyes that, although they appeared soft behind the lens of his glasses, spoke of intelligence and a certain wariness of life.

"Gina! I thought I recognized that voice. When did you get up here? Have you been by the store yet? Lucy must be workin' today. I thought I heard her leave early this mornin'."

"Yes, we've already been by the store, and yeah, she's there. I introduced her to Jo earlier, now it's your turn."

"Jo Felsenthal, meet Bob Logan. Bob Logan – Jo Felsenthal."

"Hi, Bob. Very nice to meet you. I've been so surprised at all I've seen so far. When I roamed these mountains as a kid, none of this existed. It's as if a new world has landed in my mountains. I've got so much to re-discover."

"Yeah, I can only imagine how much it's changed over the last thirty years. I've only been witness to the last eight or ten."

Gina spoke up then. "Bob, Jo's retired military and she and I were the best of friends in school. She's moved back home to Polk Ridge to take care of her mom. We're spending the weekend catching up on almost forty years apart. I wanted her to meet you 'permanent' members of the RV Park."

"Retired military, eh? Well, let me say 'thank you' for your service. We owe what little freedom we have left to those of you who serve. What branch?"

"Air Force, and you are very kind. I enjoyed my years in the military – although I was never in direct combat – I owe a debt as well to the others who were."

"What'd you do, then? I thought most Air Force people were pilots or were in direct support of combat."

"I was involved in communications for the Air Force. Base to base and base to Pentagon so I very rarely even entered a combat zone. I spent most of my time on development, installation and trouble-shooting of classified communication systems and software. I wasn't a pilot."

"Oh, you're one of them 'cyber' folks. I bet that was interesting."

"Gina, did Max get to talk to her?" Bob turned toward Gina, with a rather mischievous look on his face.

"No, he was busy in the kitchen. I figure he'll save those thoughts for the campfire tonight." Gina giggled as she and Bob shared a conspiratorial look.

"What kind of questions?" Jo was quick to query.

"Oh, Max considers himself the resident 'cyber and internet' expert in these parts. I'm sure he'll have a ton of questions for a *real* expert to answer." With that, Bob deftly changed the subject.

"I gotta guide a bunch of tourists down the Buffalo River tomorrow morning in canoes. I'll probably come to the campfire, but I won't be stayin' too late. Nice to meet you Jo, see ya later tonight."

As he disappeared through the door of his camper, Gina began to explain how Bob became a part of the community.

"Bob is retired from the chemical industry. He worked for a company in south Arkansas. When he got ready to retire, he came up here looking for land to build a cabin. He stumbled upon this place while he was looking. He spent a few weeks in one of the cabins, and during those two weeks, Max talked him into managing the RV Park during the spring and summer. Bob isn't married, but since he's been up here, he and Lucy have a part-time relationship. Not long after he decided to help with the RV Park, he bought a used camper and parked it right beside her. Been there ever since. I asked Lucy, once, about her and Bob and never really got a straight answer. I figured it was better left alone. She could talk if she ever wanted too, but she has Maxine to confide in everyday, I'm just in and out."

"Well, why is he guiding tourists in canoes?"

"Oh, he only does that for something extra, something to keep him busy. Managing this RV Park isn't that hard or time consuming and I'm sure he gets bored. And let's face it, after ten years, surely it's something he knows how to do."

"Ok, Lots #3, 4, and 5 are just part-timers that come a few weeks and weekends during the summer. I don't really know them. Next up, is Lot #6 – Aaron Hall."

"Mm… it doesn't look like Aaron's here. Oh, well, at any rate, I can tell you his story. He's from Missouri and he's an electrician. He's pretty close to our age and retired from running his own company. As I recall, he sold it. Married twice, no kids, and no desire to live anywhere close to a 'metropolitan' area. He and Bob met during a hiking retreat that Aaron attended five or six years ago. I think Aaron wanted to go canoeing while he was here? Yes, I'm pretty sure that's how they met. Anyway, at that time Max was having problems with the smoker and the electrical panel that turns the carousel. Bob and Aaron got to talking, and the next thing you know, he's at the store working on the smoker for Max. He stays for several days to help Max and then goes home. At the end of the summer, he shows up with a brand new Bighorn camper and an electrician's license for Arkansas. Bingo – another member of the community arrived!"

"Don't you just love how chaotic life can be? You never know what's right around the bend."

"No, as I recall, I don't deal too well with chaotic, Gina. Most of my adult life has been structured, timed, and disciplined. Not very much was left to chance or the unknown." Jo sighed. "I'm afraid it might be too late for me to appreciate 'a chaotic, spontaneous, or otherwise unknown' course in my life."

"Nonsense, Jo. There's no way that everything in your life was planned and anticipated. It's not possible, not even in the world of the military."

As they arrived at the jeep, Gina abruptly changed the conversation's direction. She was so darn good at jumping from one thing to another in conversation.

"Now, let's go revisit the Lost Valley Trail, and see if I still have to beg you to slow down like I used to!" The two women laughed at the thought of those teenage memories and the warmth of the friendship they had shared. They looked forward to finding those same girls in the women of today.

Maybe there *was* hope for a renewed friendship… maybe it would still be exactly as it was…

They took half an hour to arrive at the trailhead for the Lost Valley Trail. As they approached, there were already twenty-plus vehicles parked in the area reserved for hikers.

"Well, at least we won't be alone, should we run into another four legged creature we can't avoid. We'll have hope of rescue from the other hikers." Gina once again chuckled at the thought of their morning's encounter.

Jo parked the Jeep underneath the shade provided by the trees that lined the parking area. Lost in conversation, the two women gathered their hiking gear: walking sticks, backpack, and cellphones.

"We won't have much service in here, but I want to get a few pictures. It's been so long since I hiked this trail, it's bound to have changed right along with everything else. Mom will enjoy looking at them as well; especially since she's been so confined with the broken leg."

"Yeah, it's changed since you were here. They've added a few features that make it easier on the first part of the trail, it's more level than it used to be. But the last leg of the trail to Eden Falls is still rough terrain. You sure you're up to this?"

"Listen, Gina, it says 'moderate' hike. How hard can that be? I've stayed in shape by hiking in D.C. I got this."

"Ok, just reminding you – the trail ascends really quickly – it's gonna be steep," and she grinned at Jo. "Particularly for a smoker. It might be too much."

"Ha Ha, funny girl. Let's see if you can keep up any better now than you did in '76!"

Laughter ensued, and the sound of their voices, as well as the laughter floated through the mountain air, as they disappeared down the trail. Jo stopped as they entered to take a picture of the sign at the trailhead. The small act of the picture reminded Gina that she needed to share the "scrapbook" with Jo. It was a surprise she and Maureen had put together for Jo when she finally decided to come home.

No, I'll wait til we're with Maureen that would only be right.

"Hey, slowpoke, you comin'?"

The minute they were on the trail, and completely engulfed by the shade of the trees and the silence of the forest, the temperature dropped. There was an immediate coolness in the air. Jo experienced a moment of reverence for the beauty that surrounded them.

The path had been leveled by boxing that created huge squares on the path itself and had been filled with a powdery substance mixed with stone. Add a little time, a few rain storms and you had a solid, stone path. It looked and felt as though you were walking on a cobblestone surface. Benches had been placed every several hundred feet, and it seemed to Jo that everything had been done to make it a great experience for adults and children alike.

"They've done a great job with this trail. It's nothing like I remembered. In fact, this is an easy walk. It gives you a chance to soak up the beauty around you and contemplate."

"Oh yeah, the start of the trail is great. But the closer you get to the end, the more original it remains. And you're right, the Park service has done a great job when it comes to accessibility. They have school groups, daycares, visitors of all ages can come and at least make it to Natural Bridge. That's where the waterfall comes out of the bluff."

"It's the cave that many of the visitors don't make it to. It's still such a steep climb. Do you remember when Paul got stuck in the cave? When the four of us came up here to hike? As I recall, Paul never hiked this trail. But I bet he sure didn't forget it after that panic attack. I was sure he was gonna hurt himself trying to get out; I had no idea he didn't like close places, did you? He pure panicked at the back of that cave!"

Jo laughed at the memory of Paul flailing then falling all over himself to escape.

"I know it's not funny, and I didn't know he was claustrophobic, but he sure was a sight to behold rocketing out of that cave."

"I haven't kept up with Paul all these years, I only found him by accident on a website advertising 'Arkansas Wines'. Do you know what he's done with himself? Who did he marry? Has he got any kids?"

"Well of course, I know what he's done. Remember that population sign? In a town as small as Polk Ridge, you can't avoid knowing what everybody's done. Those that still live here and those that don't. Paul left long enough to attend college in Missouri. The University of Missouri, School of Business, to be exact. Shelley Atwater followed him right on up there, and in less than two years, they were married."

"Shelley? And Paul? Really? I would've never figured that. Gloria possibly, but not Shelley."

"Well, you wouldn't be the only one that never figured that. Neither did Paul's momma and daddy. They were married before Julie and Mark Collections knew the first thing. Of course, nine months later, we all figured it out!"

"Oh, no! I hate that for Paul. I don't think that's the way he pictured his life when we were graduating."

"Oh, no, it wasn't. He stayed another year at college and Shelley came home to live with his parents. Paul graduated with a degree in three years and came right back home. Home to deal with a wife, a baby, and really upset parents. It wasn't what they wanted for Paul and in the end, it wasn't what Paul wanted. Anyway, in a couple of years, there was another little Paul on the way. Fifteen years later, Shelley was on her way out. I don't guess they ever really found a way to be happy, Jo. They were absolutely too different. Shelley came from a family that believed all alcohol to be 'the work of Satan', and how she ever thought that wouldn't be an issue, is beyond me. I think she found stability and a decent life in Paul. After years of differences and arguments between them, Shelley finally decided it wasn't enough."

"So he's divorced?"

"Well, yes and no. Yes, he's divorced from Shelley, but he remarried a couple of years later. I don't know the woman he married the second time. She's from somewhere out in California. As I recall, he met her through the wine industry."

"Anyway, they lived together for four, almost five years and she went back to California. Now, I think they're legally separated. I don't think either one wanted to file for divorce, they just couldn't live together."

"What a mess! Do you ever see him now? At first, I didn't recognize his voice when I talked to him. I wasn't expecting Paul to have rental property."

"Well, I haven't run across Paul in a couple of years. He's grown the family wine business into something international, and he's not around as much as he used to be. Yes, I knew they had the rental cabins, but he usually doesn't take care of them personally. I don't know how it was that he called you."

"Maybe because I wanted to rent or lease one for several months, not for the week or weekend. The receptionist that answered my first call said she'd have someone call me back. It's possible that was why he called. She had to ask him and he only knew one Jo Felsenthal."

"Maybe, or he wanted to see what you were doin'; figure out if you were finally ready to come home." Gina's look reminded Jo that there was a past with Paul that not everyone had forgotten, not even Paul.

"Well, he never asked any personal questions. He did say it would be good to see me again. I recall he said he'd be in California for the next several months, and that was in December. I haven't had a call or an email since that conversation. He gave me his cell, but I don't really have a reason to call. None other than to catchup and I haven't been too sure I wanted to revisit those days with Paul."

As they talked, they walked. Jo had hoped that Gina would share her thoughts on visiting with Paul. The waterfall interrupted the conversation. The waterfall cascaded in fullness, falling with force against the rocks. In the spring, it flowed in abundance and sure enough the pool of water that had collected at the bottom was a beautiful lucid blue.

"Wow! Beautiful, isn't it? Let's stop and rest here for a minute and get a drink of water."

As she set the backpack on a big rock beside the trail, she reached inside for the water. Jo reached for a smoke.

"Hey, you can't smoke in a National Forest, it's against government regulations."

"What the hell -- who's gonna tell the government I smoked a cigarette? You? Who you gonna tell? Smokey the Bear?"

Gina's laughter filled the silence of the woods and echoed off the bluff walls.

"That's gonna hinder you in a few minutes. Cause from here on out, it's steep; really steep. You'll be huffin' and puffin' before you get to the cave."

"You just don't worry when it comes to my huffin' and puffin'. You worry about keeping up, Gina Ingram."

In that moment of magic, the two women returned to the girls of yesterday. Jo reverted to the name she had known for Gina all those years ago. It rolled off her lips as naturally as the water that flowed from the bluff.

"It's been awhile since anybody called me 'Gina Ingram'. Weird, but kinda nice. You had to reach way back in time for that!"

"Yeah, I suppose it's easy for me to forget it's not Ingram anymore, it's … oh wait… is it Kroon yet?"

"No, smartass, it's not Kroon yet. And it may never be Kroon; the jury's still out on that."

"C'mon Jo, quit yapping, let's finish the rest of the trail, you won't be able to talk and finish this climb." Gina snatched up the backpack, and away she went, turning to grin at Jo as she left her to follow.

CHAPTER 3

My hands were steady
My eyes were clear and bright
My walk had purpose
My steps were quick and light
And I held firmly
To what I felt was right
Like a rock…..

Bob Seger

GINA HADN'T EXAGGERATED. THE steep incline of the final leg of the trail was a series of stone steps, and Jo silently gave thanks for those stones. It was straight up, and had she been on a dirt path with loose rock or roots, she wasn't so sure she'd have made the climb.

As they reached Cob Cave, Gina threw the backpack to the ground and reached for the water.

"Time to rest a minute, it gets even steeper from here."

Jo was a good twenty feet behind. She gasped for air as she reached Gina.

"Dear Jesus, I don't remember it being this difficult. Are you sure this is the trail of our youth? They've made it longer and steeper since those days."

"Yeah, right. *They* haven't done anything to the trail, it's the years and the smoking that's hindering you. I thought you hiked in D.C. Not quite the same, eh?"

"No, not quite. Alright, I'm a wuss… I give…"

Gina smiled and offered Jo the water.

"We can rest a few minutes. We're right here at Cob Cave, and we're not on a schedule. Let's sit and chat for a little while. Let you catch your breath."

"Good gracious, I should be the one in great shape, I've spent years in the military, you've spent years as a mom and a housewife, this is ridiculous!"

Something in Jo's words struck a nerve in Gina. Her face turned a bright crimson.

"Now just what do you mean by that? Housewives aren't as healthy as career military women?"

"No, I truly only meant that I've been through PT drills and all sorts of physical strength testing, you haven't. Looks like I wouldn't be so pathetically give out from a simple hike."

"I've been hiking these mountains all the years you've been gone. I never quit hiking and walking; and running after kids will do a lot to keep you in shape."

Jo sensed that the conversation was not headed in the right direction, or with the right tone.

How did this become laced with an undercurrent?

"Let me ask you something, Jo. Something I've been wanting to ask ever since 1976. Did it ever once cross your mind that I really missed you? That I felt like you abandoned me when I needed you most? I loved you like a sister, or as much as I could figure what that was like. And you just left. I know my life was a mess, but I needed you to help me through that mess. Why did you change so much when you left? Why was there no time for us anymore?"

Now, I know. Now we get to the real issue.

Jo was silent for several minutes. Emotions played across her face. She needed to find the right words to answer Gina, without having to tell the whole story. She just wasn't ready yet.

"Gina," her voice was low and measured, "I guess I didn't view life from that perspective. I never meant to leave you abandoned, or alone. There were so many things changing in my life, so many things that left me confused and unsure of my own place in life. I couldn't comfort anybody, not even you."

They sat silently for another few minutes.

Jo finally spoke again.

"We made decisions, really without even realizing the consequences. We just did it, and looking back, I realize it tore us apart. But I don't think either one of us realized we'd travel in such different directions. You never thought you'd be getting pregnant. I know I sure as hell didn't consider that the military would be as hard as it turned out to be; those things didn't leave us time or room for each other. Not for a long time."

Gina sat silently for several minutes, and Jo was beginning to wonder if her friend was going to speak, or simply stand up and leave.

"I guess there's truth in that. I never occurred to me to consider your life as being hard. I guess I thought it was always so worldly and in a weird way, kind of glamourous; Jo, the 'military genius'; traveling and seeing the world. I've spent more than a few years resenting that. Here I was stuck in Polk Ridge, a housewife for so many years. I guess I let myself get lost in feeling sorry for myself. We've been such different people, with different lives for so long. I never gave much thought to the impact of all those differences on the 'us' of today."

"Yes, we have been in different places, and lived different lives. But that doesn't mean we can't try to pick up the pieces. We have so much history and so many memories. Surely it's worth a try to find the friendship we once had, too."

Sweat dripped from their faces and drenched their clothes. But they both experienced a definite chill. There were many differences and emotions to overcome.

Finally, it was Gina that extended the olive branch.

"C'mon, we've still got a quarter mile before we reach Eden Falls, we don't have to sort everything out in one afternoon. We do however, have to be outta here by 6pm. It's gonna be close by the time we get back."

Jo hadn't even bothered to reach for a smoke. She'd been too busy sucking in several lungs full of air, trying to prepare her aching body for the last quarter mile.

Conversation was sparse as the two women covered the last leg of their hike. Neither was sure if it was the physical exertion or the tense moments at the cave. Silence seemed to be preferable at the moment.

At last, Gina called out to Jo, "Hurry up, I see Eden Falls, and the big cave. I swear, Jo, you're as slow as cream rising on buttermilk nowadays."

Hurry up hell, this is as fast as it gets at this point.

There was a small space at the base of Eden Falls where they could sit, rest and admire the beauty of the cascading waterfall.

Gina once again unpacked the water, and pack of Tom's crackers she'd stuffed in the backpack before they left home that morning.

"You wanna cracker?"

"No, I'm just dying of thirst."

"I know it's gorgeous here, but now I'm not sure if it's the sheer beauty of the place or pure and simple relief. Relief that I finally get to sit down and rest that makes it so pretty."

Gina began to laugh.

"At our age, it's both. Look, I'm sorry. I guess I've harbored more resentment than I realized; there's no fault to find between us. We've just lived different lives. And you're right, that shouldn't keep us from trying to find the kind of friendship we had before."

"Life is all about compromise. At seventeen, it's black and white. By 50, it's all gray areas, and I'm not referring to the hair, either!"

Laughter from both of them filled the silence of the woods, and the mood lightened. Apparently, there was something worth salvaging.

They spent another thirty minutes or so basking in the beauty of the waterfall. The falls were framed by green foliage that clung tenaciously to the bluff and rock walls. Sunshine danced through small openings between the towering canopies of leaves from the beech trees. And Jo made picture after picture. Some of them with Gina posing beside the sign that read "Eden Falls", but most of them of the surrounding mountain scenery. She would enjoy sharing these with Maggie and George. Almost as much as she enjoyed sharing the moment with Gina.

Finally, after the picture taking was finished, and both women had rested, it was time for the return descent.

Jo hadn't noticed how many of the final stones were moss covered and slick on her way up, now however, coming down, it was harder to balance and navigate. More than once her feet slipped on the stones.

The stones that completed the path to Eden Falls, and the cave, had spent lots of years collecting the spray from the waterfall and the moisture. It had created a perfect home for the greenest moss Jo had ever seen. It was also the slickest.

"Gina, you've got to slow down and wait. I can't keep up… I'd forgotten the real meaning of 'moderate hike'."

Jo's breathing gave her away. No matter how many hikes she and Maggie and George had made through Rock Park, she wasn't prepared for the Ozarks.

"Jo, I seem to remember a day when I was the one asking for someone to wait; Mm… we've once again switched roles."

There was laughter lacing Gina's comment, and a twinkle in her eye as she stopped to wait on her hiking companion and best friend. She looked back barely in time to witness Jo completely lose her footing on the slippery, mold covered stones of the upper portion of the Lost Valley Trail.

As the scene unfolded, Gina felt as though she was watching a movie in slow motion. Jo's less than graceful attempt to re-balance herself and regain her footing, only served to add momentum to the fall. A fall that was as inevitable as the increasing shadows of the Ozarks in the late afternoon sun.

The scream that came from Jo's mouth was released from lungs already laboring to accommodate her physical need for oxygen. The sound was a cross between the howl of a bear cub in distress and the screech of a night owl. If Gina hadn't been so concerned for her friend's safety, she might have burst into immediate laughter. As it turns out, the laughter did come. But only after she watched her friend roll several feet down the side of the trail and into the crevice of boulders that were clumped together. They appeared to be waiting for the sole purpose of cradling Jo's crumpled form.

As Gina scrambled to her friend's side, she pondered the thought that this might just turn into a summer she would never forget.

"Jo! Jo! Are you alright? Did you break anything? Can you stand up?"

Gina fired questions faster than a Gatling gun could spray bullets.

A dazed and disheveled Jo raised her head from the pile of leaves and dirt that had accumulated underneath her as she plowed over the ground.

"Oh… oh… my ankle, my leg…"

"Can you stand up?"

"Oh crap, my ankle hurts like hell. No, I don't think anything's broken. My arm is scraped. So is my left leg, they're burnin' like fire.

Oh no, easy… easy. I can't stand up on my ankle. Oh, shit, please tell me it's not broken."

"Here, lean against this rock. See if you can help me pull you up. There you go, slow… slow… not too fast."

"Now, lean right there a minute, and let me look at your arm. Yep, it's scraped and bruised. You wanna shed your pants and let me look at your leg?"

"No, I don't wanna drop my pants, there's no blood on my jeans. It can wait till we get back to the cabin."

"Well, your hair's a mess, and you got more dirt on your face than you left on the ground." She giggled as she tried to control the laughter.

"Gee thanks for the cosmetic update. I'm glad you think it's so funny. Let me try to stand on this ankle."

Jo gingerly applied pressure to her ankle as she tried to stand on it. Although it really hurt, it wasn't impossible for her stand.

"Well, it may take a little while, but I should be able to walk on it; it won't be as quick a descent as we thought though. What time is it? Have we got enough time to make it back before dark?"

"Yeah, it's only 4. It shouldn't take us more than an hour or so to get back to the Jeep, even at a slow pace. Here, let me get this walking stick out of the backpack; you can use it for balance and to relieve your weight on that foot."

She fished around in the backpack for the expanding stick as Jo fidgeted with first her hair, then her shirt. She tried to shake the leaves from the mass of hair that at the moment resembled a mop more than a hairdo.

"I really am a mess, aren't I? That was a scary ride. Once I got started, I couldn't get myself straightened out. I basically had to let it go and curl up, hoping something would catch my fall."

"If I hadn't been so worried, I would've laughed at the sight of you in a ball, rolling around in the woods Jo. It was pretty funny as you rolled down the side of the hill."

"So much for worry and concern. I noticed it didn't take you but two seconds to get down here and see if I was alright though."

"I couldn't very well explain how I dragged you off to the mountains for the weekend, only to let you kill yourself. Nobody would believe you fallin' off the side of one of them. I could see the sheriff now: "Gina, you sure she just fell?" Better to make sure you were at least conscious." Mirth once again threatened to bubble up out of Gina.

"Ok, let's try to get out of here without another mishap. C'mon, you can lean against me till we get to more level ground. There's enough room to walk side by side the rest of the way down the stones."

Jo gave her best announcer's voice.

"Twiddle Dee and Twiddle Dum comin' through folks, step aside, step aside." This time real laughter erupted from Gina, and Jo couldn't help but join her.

What the hell? I don't think I broke anything. Might as well laugh instead of cry.

Jo turned to look back at her landing place. Only then did she notice that had she fallen just a little more to the right, she would have tumbled another thirty or forty feet. The next thirty or forty was a much steeper drop, with nothing to catch her at all.

She shuddered, and the woman of today realized it could have been much worse. She could have *really* been hurt. This brought another thought.

"Gina, there's something else I need to tell you, and I really need to tell you before I fall again and break my neck. You need to know a little more concerning what happened when I left here and went to the Academy. It might help you to understand why I was so distant, so removed from Polk Ridge."

"When I got to the Academy, I was scared to death. I'd never been anywhere like a military base. I didn't know anybody; you know you were supposed to go with me. After a couple of weeks, I met Maggie Wilson. I made a friend in Maggie Wilson and she helped me through the time at Jack Valley. Jack Valley, something I've tried hard to deal with and move past. But you need to know; you need to know because it affected me and that in turn affected you. About halfway through our BCT…."

Jo walked as she talked and shared with Gina the events of the night at Jack Valley in the mountains of Colorado. Something she had never shared with any other human being, except Maggie.

A stunned Gina simply stopped and stared at Jo.

"You were raped? Why didn't you tell somebody? Why didn't they do something?"

It was evident that Gina was having trouble absorbing what Jo had revealed and fired questions faster than Jo could supply answers.

"Hang on. I didn't tell anyone for a very good reason. Listen for a minute and you'll begin to understand."

"I didn't report it because the very ones who did that, would've won, Gina. Reporting a rape simply helped prove the argument behind never allowing us into the Academy in the first place. Yes, I had been assaulted, and that was horrible, but I was still a cadet. I wasn't giving that up for anyone or for any reason. That would've made everything harder for me. Then, everything I worked for would have been lost."

"Oh, Jo. I had no idea. No wonder you didn't call or write. God, you were too busy just trying to cope. And no, I couldn't have begun to understand what you were going through. Nor could you understand what I was dealing with. How did it go so awry? We had such great plans; we had it all figured out."

"No, we didn't. We only thought we did. You've seen the yellow bumper sticker, 'Shit happens'? Life just happens Gina. When you're young, shit just happens. You *react* to life, not the other way around. Then, as you get older, you prepare, plan and anticipate; you don't do that when you're young. You roll with the punches and wait for the next big adventure."

Although it had taken longer than the hour and half Gina had first thought, they slowly reached the end of the trail. Gina was the first to spot the jeep as they came out from the cover of the National Forest. The day was fading into shadows and was even more pronounced surrounded by the cover of a canopy of green leaves and walls of tree trunks. To Jo, it was as if she were emerging from a forgotten time and place; for Gina it was a comfortable familiarity – the Ozarks she loved in the company of a friend she had missed for so long.

And for them both, so much more ground had been covered than the physical distance of that two mile hike.

Questions had been answered, but so many still remained. The one thing it seemed they had determined: there was at least a reason to try... they were still able to talk, even disagree and find common ground. How much was black, how much was white, and how much was gray, was yet to be determined.

CHAPTER 4

John Denver

ONCE THEY REACHED THE jeep, Gina demanded the keys.

"Where'd you put the keys? You know you're not gonna drive us back to the cabin. Even if your ankle isn't broken, you're not in any shape to drive. You need a nice hot shower and a glass of wine. The wine will take the edge off so you can get some rest. Even if there's nothing broken, you're gonna hurt tonight."

Jo groaned. She hadn't even given thought to the aching she might experience at 1 o'clock in the morning.

"I didn't bring a thing for pain. You're right, even if nothing's broken, it's gonna hurt like hell later tonight."

"See? I told you this weekend would endanger something, I was right. That trek up the trail has damn near killed me, I don't even wanna talk about ziplining tomorrow. It'll be a miracle if I can even move in the morning. Fifty year old bones don't bounce back overnight."

Gina snorted. "Quit looking for an excuse not to go. Why don't we just wait and see? I don't think there's that much damage. Yes, you're a tad bit scuffed up, but your ankle's not even swelling. You're just bein' a chicken, Jo. You sure you didn't plan that roll down the hill, so you won't have to try ziplining?"

Jo gave her a stare. Same old Gina, she knew exactly how to push Jo's buttons. And she could still spot a stall a mile away.

"Fine. We'll wait. But how am I supposed to zipline with a bum ankle? I may not have tried this ridiculous sport, but I know you have to catch yourself when you reach the end of the line."

"Yes, you do, but it's not what you're thinking. You don't 'land' on your feet, so much as you're caught by the guides."

"Caught? They catch you? What are we, the flying Wallendas'? Caught? You have to land on something."

This time, Gina laughed outright.

"You're making this more complicated than it really is. Wait and see for yourself tomorrow. You'll be able to master a little ole' zipline, Jo. Surely that military training will kick in. Didn't you learn to "adapt and overcome"? What's a bruise or two, when you have a chance at high flyin' adventure?"

Just as Jo was searching for a scathing comment about the 'adapt and overcome' thought, they rounded a curve in the road. And once again, she was surprised by the little community that lay before her.

"Ok, here we are, Cabin 2 is right over there, and if I know Maxine, she's been over unlocked it, and gotten it ready for us. We'll go there first; if it's not ready, I can walk over to the store. You don't need to get out til you can get in the cabin and take a shower."

Gina carefully navigated the gravel lot and drive to Cabin 2, trying her best not to unseat Jo or move her unnecessarily. Finally, she stopped the jeep right beside the door to the cabin. As she had predicted, it was unlocked.

The cabin was made entirely of logs with a set of log steps that led up the side and to the door. Next, Jo surveyed the deck. It spanned the entire width of the cabin. The deck came furnished with a grill, two chairs and a table, and a bird feeder fully stocked for the various feathered guests. Jo guessed their feathered friends would be in abundant supply.

Once inside, it closely resembled the cabin Jo occupied in Polk Ridge. The kitchen and living room were one open spacious room. A short hall divided the left and right sides of the cabin. The first door on the right opened into the bathroom, and further back, a second door led to a bedroom; on the left, there was simply one big bedroom. Furnishings were sparse, but aptly met the needs of visitors or couples on a weekend retreat.

With Gina's help, Jo made it up the few steps and into the waiting plushness of the sofa.

"Alright, you have a seat and let me get everything out of the jeep. When I finish, we'll try to get you in the shower."

Jo groaned as she lowered herself to the couch, she hurt all over. This was going to be a long night. Gina busied herself for the next few minutes hauling luggage and backpacks from the jeep to the cabin while Jo could only sit and watch.

"You know, if you wanted a bell hop for all this crap you brought, you didn't have to fall and nearly kill yourself. You could've just asked… and why on earth did you bring so much stuff? We're only gonna be here for two days; not two weeks."

"Only you would volunteer to unload it, and then fuss because there's so much *to* unload. I didn't intend to unload everything, but you never asked. It didn't cross my mind until you came in with all those bags."

"Bang your head, did you? Amnesia settin' in?" Gina asked with a big grin. "I bet Maxine's probably got a Chardonnay that will be exactly what you need to alleviate the suffering. Let's get you into the shower. Then I'll run over to the store, pick up supper, and get something 'medicinal' for you to drink."

She helped Jo to her feet, and was moving to aid with her walk to the shower, when Jo shooed her away.

"I can walk! I just can't get up and down very well. Go on over to the store. It's nearly seven and I'm starving. Remember, we only had a light lunch and nothing while we were hiking. How late are they open over there? What have they got to eat?"

"Well, apparently the fall didn't affect your appetite. You've got no problem asking questions, or demanding answers when it comes to food! They're open til 8, and we can choose from BBQ, or BBQ, or BBQ." She grinned at Jo, "Do you like either of those?"

As Gina grabbed her purse and keys, Jo moved slowly and with great effort towards the bathroom and the certain relief of a hot shower.

"I'll grab some drinks, and a bottle of wine from Maxine, you want anything else?"

"Yeah, bring me back a pack of cigarettes, this may be a long night."

"I'll ask Maxine if she's got anything at the store for pain, too, in case you need something later tonight. I may visit with them for a few minutes, so don't look for me to be back until around 8; it'll take them a little while to get our supper ready, anyway." With that, Jo heard her friend slam the door to the cabin, she was already slowly removing dirt-covered clothing, and watching as the steam filled the shower. *Oh, blessed hot water, relief was in sight.*

As Jo peeled away the clothing, there were a few more bruises than she expected. The one on her arm and the one on her leg, however, were nice big purple splotches; the bruises shared their space on her limbs with claw-like scrapes. Stones and rocks could be so unyielding when forced against unsuspecting and crashing flesh.

The bruise on her leg, wasn't quite as bad as she had worried. But the bruise on her arm, was plump from swelling and more than a little feverish. Both places would hurt before the night was very old.

True to her word, it was fully 8 o'clock before she returned. Jo had finished in the shower and lay stretched out on the couch in pajamas.

"God, that smells good; I'm starving! What did you get besides BBQ? It smells really good."

"I got some baked beans and potato salad. I didn't know if you liked them, but they go great with BBQ and Maxine's potato salad is to die for. Come on over to the table, I'll set it all out."

Jo slowly raised herself from the couch.

"Well, what was the damage? You gonna live?"

"Yeah, other than a couple of purple bruises and some scraped places on my arm and leg, the ankle is the only thing that still really hurts. It's not swellin' though, apparently I just turned it over when I started to fall."

They sat down to the feast Gina had laid out on the table and hunger overtook conversation for several minutes.

At one point during the meal, Jo sniffed the air around the table.

"What kind of wood do they use to smoke this BBQ? It's got a funny smell, or perhaps it's some of her seasoning."

"I don't know… I've never noticed anything unusual and I've never asked Max much when it comes to his smoking-slash- cooking process. He's so secretive. Do you suppose it's your sniffer, reckon you damaged your nose when you fell?" She laughed, but kept her face lowered to her food. She was really hungry as well.

"Let me fix you a glass of the wine Maxine sent. That oughta help you overcome the stiffness, or at least temporarily forget it. She sent some kinda homemade remedy for your soreness, too. She said take a couple of teaspoons with a glass of water. You oughta sleep like a baby and be rested. Not so sore in the morning."

"I'm not takin' some kind of 'homemade remedy' without knowing what's in it. I don't care who made it."

"Oh, my goodness, Jo. It ain't gonna hurt you! Just take a couple of teaspoons, like she said. I don't know what she puts in it, but it works. I've taken it myself."

"No, I'm not takin it. I still wonder what he uses on this BBQ. I can't put my finger on that smell…"

"Well, we can ask him tonight, if you wanna go to the campfire, or you can ask him in the mornin', if you don't. You feel like goin' for a little while?"

"Hell no, I'm not goin' anywhere. I'm gonna finish eating and go to bed and pray I'm better in the morning. You actually wanna go sit around a campfire? This late?"

"Well, yeah. I always go. Besides, I didn't fall off the side of a mountain this afternoon. You did. I really wanted you to go and get to know everybody we met today. But I guess if you don't feel like it there's always the next time we come up here. We've got all summer for you to get to know these folks, anyway."

At this point in the conversation, both had finished their plates and Gina got up to clear the table.

"Well, I'll leave the stuff Maxine sent settin' on the counter, in case you change your mind. I won't stay long, maybe til 10 or so. You'll probably be asleep by the time I get back. Take that bedroom on the left down the hall, it's closest to the bathroom and the kitchen. I'll check in on you when I get back."

Jo had reached the couch, nursing her glass of wine, and taking the bottle of Chardonnay with her.

"I'll be fine, go on and visit with your friends. I'm almost ready to call it a night anyway."

She wanted time to think about their hike today. Although they had talked over so many things, Jo still felt as though she was getting to know a stranger; a stranger that wasn't as easy to learn as the fifteen year old she remembered from her youth.

And to make matters worse, some part of her felt as though she was a stranger in her own homeland. These were still the same mountains of her youth, but so much had changed. So many of the people she'd met today didn't grow up here. They had different lifestyles, and no doubt different opinions when it came to so many of the ideals and beliefs she held so dear.

Gina was a product of a life lived surrounded by the mountains: mountain beliefs and mountain ways of life. Jo still held a fondness and respect for the mountains and a deep love of her childhood. But she wondered how the differences in their lives might affect their efforts at friendship today.

I've missed Gina, the Gina I once knew. The reality is though, the Gina of today isn't the same as the Gina of yesterday. She's so trusting of all these people; just like the 'homemade remedy' – how long since I even thought about mountain remedies, much less took any? What does she really know about them? They're from everywhere. What's lurking in their past? How can we move forward if we share totally different views on life?

The chardonnay took effect and Jo abandoned her thoughts to give herself over to a restless, short sleep.

As Gina left the cabin, her thoughts too turned to a sobering reality. The reality that there was still a lot to overcome if they were going to be able to call themselves "best friends" again.

Poor, Jo. She's become so cynical, I've no doubt she's not as enamored with these mountain folks as I am. I can't believe she's changed so much. And I know that livin' all over the world is vastly different than livin' right here surrounded by family and friends. There's goin' to be things we'll have to overcome; Many of my views won't be hers... I only hope there's enough left of what we once had to find a way...

She had walked the short distance over to the blaze she'd seen from the cabin. She loved this simple fellowship. It was such a great chance to enjoy others' company, relax, talk and laugh. Too bad Jo doesn't.

"Hey, guys. Finally got the patient tended to, but she didn't feel like comin'."

She plopped down Indian-style with the others already seated around the campfire.

"What's the topic right now? Government interference? Stories relating to the weekenders? Who's got the floor? Do I smell a skunk?"

It wasn't long before Gina was fully immersed in the conversation, the laughter and the billowing, blowing smoke.

It was Max that brought the conversation around to Jo, and her military background. He quizzed Gina.

"You didn't mention that Jo was a Major in the Air Force before today and neither of you have volunteered any information connected to what she does."

"Because she's retired."

"What *did* she do while she was in the military?"

"Well, I didn't volunteer any information because I figured she would have a chance to tell you herself. And besides, a lot of what she did I really don't understand. She did ask me if you guys might know her friend she worked with in D.C.; I recall his name is George. George Durand?"

Max looked as if he'd seen a ghost, and sucked in so much air, everyone thought he might choke on the smoke.

"*She* worked with George? For those immoral, disrespecting, disgusting government spies? *She* was with cybersecurity and all that NSA bunch that spies on us?"

Gina looked taken aback.

"So you do know George? How do you… is he…"

Before she could finish, and Max could launch into the rest of his anti-government speech, Maxine injected herself into the conversation.

"Yes, Gina. George is our son. We don't necessarily agree with many of the things that our government does, but George is a son we're proud of. He is really good at what he does and he's devoted himself to the security he believes is so crucial to keeping us safe."

"I guess I didn't realize you had *two* sons. I know Lucas, I've met him here before when he came to visit you guys last year; but you never mentioned another son."

"Well, we don't mention George much, mostly because Max gets so worked up over what he does in Washington."

At that moment, Max had recovered sufficiently to return to the conversation.

"Just because I don't agree, Maxine, doesn't mean I'm not proud of him. I don't think spying on your own citizens is necessary to keep us safe. It's another way to control us. And it certainly can't be in keeping with our Constitution, I don't care what them fancy pants in Washington say."

"Well, Jo really thinks the world of George. She said they worked together for 10 years or so in D.C. I still don't understand all the stuff Jo tried to explain what they did, but it sounded really technical and really important. You'll have to wait and talk to her."

Bob sat silently during the exchange. He had figured out more about Jo in their ten-minute conversation that morning than he cared to discuss. She might be Gina's friend, but her life had been spent engaging in activity he tried really hard to keep out of his life. This was going to be an interesting summer.

Gina wasn't going to let him escape the conversation so easily.

"Bob, you met her this morning, she told you what she does. What's your opinion? Do you think they spy on us?"

It took Bob a few minutes to respond. For a few seconds, she wondered if he had heard her.

"Well, I guess that George and Jo believe in what they do, or did. What George is still doin'g. Do I believe cybersecurity is necessary to keep our enemies in check? Absolutely. Do I believe that they're also spying on us? Absolutely. There's just no clear cut answer here. Time will tell if Jo can understand our position, and if we can understand hers."

Gina sat silently. *That pretty much summed up where she and Jo were. Only time would tell if they could meet somewhere in the middle; somewhere to be close friends once again.*

Around 10, she bid her friends goodbye.

"We've got an appointment to go ziplining in the morning, and I'm not gonna miss that. Especially with Jo. She's already decided she might die while she's high flyin over the Ozarks; comical probably won't really describe this show. Good-night everybody. See ya tomorrow".

She slipped through the door of the cabin as quietly as she could manage and noticed Jo had left the light on over the stove. The half-empty bottle of Chardonnay on the table beside the couch. Maxine's "remedy" untouched.

She stopped in the living room long enough to remove her tennis shoes and padded down the hallway to peep in on Jo. She was sound asleep.

Gina smiled to herself. Some things never changed. Jo lay fast asleep. One leg under the covers, one on top. She always slept so funny. What difference did it make where your legs were? Jo had always slept that way, even as a kid. The more amusing part of that knowledge for Gina, was the fact that Millie did too. Millie, her "Jo-like" daughter had so much in common with a woman she barely knew.

She stumbled the rest of the way to her waiting bed. Ah, blissful sleep….

A foggy morning mist covered the mountain tops and greeted the women as they pulled themselves from their slumber. Gina heard Jo in the bathroom as she made her way down the hallway into the kitchen. Time for coffee, toast, and a few minutes to clear the spider webs from her mind.

She pulled the coffee from the cabinet and measured out enough for a full pot. As she did, she noticed the teaspoon and the home remedy Maxine had given her were still sitting on the counter; but the bottle wasn't full. She grinned. Apparently, Jo wasn't as removed from the mountain folk "remedies" as she thought.

Jo came down the hallway.

"Good morning, Sunshine. I'm making coffee; I don't know about you, but I gotta have some caffeine for this foggy head. Did you rest okay last night?"

A less than stellar looking Jo stared at Gina through the lens of a foggy head.

"Not until around 1 o'clock; I hurt every time I moved. Finally, I got up and took a teaspoon of that shit Maxine sent. Nasty, nasty stuff. But I didn't move again til roughly fifteen minutes ago. Whatever is in it put me out. I mean, it was lights out for the rest of the night. And, although I hate to admit it, I'm a little better this morning. My brain is mush, and I feel like I'm walking in a fog. Hurry up with that coffee, please."

She plopped down at the table and stared blankly out the massive windows that lined the exterior of the living room and kitchen wall. The fog of her mind met the fog of the mountain. It would be the better part of an hour before there were clear skies: both on the mountain and in her head.

Gina had her back to Jo, but smiled once again, to herself.

Not the happy morning person.

CHAPTER 5

'Cause I get a peaceful easy feeling
And I know you won't let me down
'Cause I'm already standing…..
I'm already standing….
Yes, I'm already standing on the ground.

Eagles

SOMEWHERE AROUND 9, THEY feasted on the toast and eggs Gina had managed to cook. All the while, they both sought the uplifting and energizing effect of the coffee.

"We've got a date at 11 to zipline, so we better get it in gear. It'll only take a few minutes to get over there, but I want to be early, not late." Gina managed to slip that small fact into the conversation as she got up with the leftovers and dirty dishes.

Jo didn't comment as she stood from the table.

"I'm going outside to smoke. Right after I refill this coffee cup."

"Ok, I'm gonna go grab a shower and call to check on Dad. I finally got everything tended to on Friday, from his little 'fender-bender'. But he was a little shook up from the accident, so I need to check on him."

"Oh, my goodness. I didn't know… what happened? We could've waited, you should have called me."

"It really wasn't that bad, he was backin' out of his driveway, and when he backed out, there was another vehicle coming down the street. Neither one of them was going very fast, they basically just didn't see each other. And of course, according to Dad, it's the other guys fault, never mind he backed out in front of him."

Jo giggled. Poor Mr. Floyd. "You weren't too hard on him Friday, were you? He's is getting old."

"Yeah, he's gettin' old, but he still has to pay attention to the traffic and traffic regulations or he can't drive. I haven't said anything yet, but we're going to have a talk about his driving, and possibly moving to an assisted living facility. He's nearly eighty years old – it's time for him to give up the drivin'."

"Good luck with that. You know what kinda fuss he's gonna put up? He's too independent to give it up."

"He may think he is, but that little wreck Friday shook him up in more ways than one."

At that very moment, Gina's phone began to ring, Mr. Floyd had beat her to the punch.

"Speaking of Dad…" and she winked at Jo.

Jo slipped out the door to sit outside on the porch and smoke her morning cigarette. She was still pondering the ziplining excursion, and searching for a way to avoid it, if at all possible.

By 9:45, a showered and dressed Gina was ready to go.

"Ok, it's all yours, as soon as you're finished gettin' ready, we're good to go. I'm so excited and it looks like so much fun. I actually went over to check it out once before when I was here, but I didn't have time to schedule a tour – now, it's time for adventure!"

If she had hoped her pep talk would inspire Jo, she was sadly mistaken.

Jo slowly extricated herself from the chair on the porch.

"Ok, I'm going to get ready. But you need to pray that I don't bruise, bang, fall, roll, drop, or otherwise meet with anything that might bring physical discomfort or harm. If I do, I can promise you there'll be no more adventures this summer!"

"Yes ma'm." Her voice was muted, but the grin that covered her face spoke volumes.

"I promise, this should be as safe as buckling up and riding in the jeep."

"You can't know that; there's no way. Anything can happen when you're hanging from a cable 80 feet off the ground. That even sounds dangerous."

"Oh, go on and get a shower – you'll see when we get there."

As they rounded a curve in the narrow mountain road, Jo saw the sign. "Tree Top Tours – Ziplining – Experience a new freedom in the Mountains of the Ozarks". There was a long arrow at the bottom of the billboard like sign that pointed towards the dirt road to her right.

Just as she read the sign, Gina's excited squeal captured her attention.

"That's it! That's where we're going! This is gonna be great! Look at that mountaintop right over there; I'll bet that's the one we're going to …. this will be awesome Jo!"

Her face was one big excited bubble of anticipation. Jo's however, was not.

She was slow to comment, and even slower to admit that Gina might be right. It did seem like an "awesome" experience, at least from the ground and her view at the moment.

Looking down from 80 feet, she might have a different perspective.

"If you say so, the jury's still out over here. I'm not making any promises, till I look at what we're jumping off of and how safe it looks."

She had turned down the narrow little dirt road and was only creeping along as if she were slowly 'walking the plank' towards certain death.

"Oh, c'mon, Jo, speed up – it's not like it's a superhighway – we're not gonna meet anyone. We gotta get there by 11, we gotta suit up, go over the procedures and safety practices, and then be ready to fly!"

"Ya know, I am still questioning my sanity over agreeing to this adventure. Please pardon me if I don't rush to the event. I need time to contemplate and study. Study on what we're fixin' to do."

"If you think long, you think wrong! Just do it! Isn't that Nike's slogan? Just do it? These folks know what they're doin', we'll be fine. Oh, and there it is!"

They reached a clearing that signaled the end of the road, and for Jo, it had a more literal meaning. A small block building sat in the middle of the clearing.

Oh, Lord, Jo thought, this looks so inadequate. Where's the ambulance, the rescue team?

"There, park right over there in the shade." Gina quipped, barely able to contain herself, and keep from leaping out of the jeep. "I'm ready!"

As if on cue, three individuals emerged from the block building waving excitedly to them.

They want us to feel welcome, not like we're fixing to die.

"C'mon Jo, get out, let's go!"

Gina was already out of the jeep and headed toward the instructors and guides.

"Hey, ladies. What a beautiful day for flying over the treetops!" She greeted them with all the enthusiasm of a released prisoner at his moment of freedom.

"Hello, are you our 11 o'clock appointment?" Gina nodded her answer of confirmation.

"We are, and we're ready to go!"

Jo was slower in arriving to meet her guides. And was much less enthusiastic when she provided her confirmation.

"Yes, we're the 11 o'clock guinea pigs. I truly hope we don't live to regret this 'adventure' Gina keeps telling me we're going to love."

"Oh, you'll be fine. These two ladies beside me will be your guides, and I'll walk you through the gear, how to suit up, and what you can expect along the way. My name is Julie, the guides are Lori and Tammy, and you would be?"

"I'm Jo Felsenthal and this is my friend Gina Phillips."

Gina was too busy surveying their surroundings and looking at the harnesses to beat Jo to the response.

"Well, alright, follow me, ladies. We'll get you started."

For the next twenty minutes, Julie covered all aspects of the zipline experience. How to put on the harnesses, how to tighten them, how to hold their hands, legs, and bodies as they flew along the cable. She explained the cable system that their harnesses would depend on to carry them from landing to landing. As well as a host of safety concerns. Such as how the zipline was inspected, the amount of weight the cable was certified to hold and how often they replaced the cables. During this explanation she also covered the number of individuals that could occupy the cable and landing at one time, and that each harness also met certain safety qualifications. At the end of her speech, and as each woman was suited up, Jo began to feel more at ease.

"Ok, everyone ready?"

Gina nodded like an excited squirrel that had found a treasure chest of nuts. Jo slowly added her confirmation nod.

"Alright then, Lori and Tammy will take you from here! See ya after your 'flight'

They followed along behind their guides down the short trail that led to the first landing spot. Gina made small talk with the guides while Jo walked in subdued silence.

Dear Lord, please let me live through this not-so-well-thought-out excursion. I know I've not been the best at praying, but I sure hope you hear me today. Amen.

As the trail ended, it opened into a large field, and right there in front of them, stood what looked to Jo like a fire tower. Made of wood, with steps that began on the left side, you first reached a platform. Once at the platform, you made a 45-degree turn and started up once again. This was repeated several times until you finally reached a height of nearly 80 feet.

Jo simply stared. Her stomach, rebelling against the thought of climbing 80 feet, lurched and flip-flopped inside her.

Oh dear, it's worse than I imagined.

If Gina had any second thoughts, it wasn't reflected in her ascent up the tower. She climbed the stairs as nimbly as a cat on a hot tin roof.

She couldn't wait to experience the zipline.

Oh, my gosh, I'm finally gonna get to zipline! This view is awesome! Only a few more minutes, and I'll be flying over the open field!

She turned to check on Jo making sure she wasn't still standing at the bottom. She was definitely moving, albeit very slowly. It was with shaky steps that she finally reached the top of the platform.

Why the hell would you jump off a perfectly good platform, held only by a cable and a harness? Why am I here? What was I thinking? Her knuckles gripped the railing as though it were all that stood between life as she knew it and certain death.

"Crap, this is high!"

"Yeah and look what a view! You wanna go first, or can I?"

"By all means, please, be my guest. You may most certainly go first. And if you don't make it across, I'll see you at the hospital." Sarcasm dripped from Jo's tongue.

Gina giggled. There was absolutely no sign of fear or apprehension anywhere on her smiling, giggling face.

"I don't know if you're extremely naïve or nuts, Gina. You do realize there's the possibility something could go wrong, right?"

"Oh, my god, Jo. Lighten up. Try to have a good time!"

"Alright, ladies, Lori will go across to show you how this is done, setup the catch on the other end, and then we'll be ready for you. Let me walk you through the process of connecting to the cable, and what I DO and DO NOT want you to do while you are connected to the cable."

As Tammy explained the connecting and take off process to them, Gina listened as though she were preparing to embark on a climb up Mount Everest. Jo listened, too overwhelmed by the height of the platform and her fear of falling to be as raptly enthralled as Gina.

"Ok, listen for Lori's 'ready' call, and then it'll be time to go."

As Lori connected her harness to the cable, she smiled, turned to them and saluted. "Here we go!" She jumped from the platform and away she went.

They could hear the "zing" of the cable, and they both watched in awe as she easily guided her harness towards the landing platform. Within a few seconds, she was safely on the other end. In another few minutes, they heard the "ready" call, and Tammy began to hook Gina's harness.

"Ready? This first one is some kinda ride; now, sit down in your harness and when you're ready, push off the platform. This cable is taking you to a much lower platform, so all you have to do is float across."

"I'm ready, 1-2-3, push!" With those few words, she was off and flying over the open field. Shrieking, laughing and hollering the entire way.

Jo watched in horror, waiting expectantly for the cable or the harness to break, or some other catastrophic event to take place that would result in Gina's demise. Nothing happened. In barely sixty seconds, she was waving from the other side.

"Ok, Miss Jo – your turn."

Jo's legs seemed to be made of concrete. They were way too heavy as she picked up her feet to move toward the cable. Her hands trembled as she grasped the harness and Tammy clicked the carabineer onto the cable.

Fear must have been evident on her face, as Tammy turned her around, because she took the time to reassure Jo.

"It really is safe, there's nothing to worry you. Most people are really skeptical and sometimes afraid on this first jump, but after you get the first one behind you, you'll relax and be much better."

"That's easy for you to say – you're not the one jumping."

Tammy gave her a smile, and then "ok, 1-2-3-go!"

Jo jumped. Time stood still. The scream that burst from her lungs consumed every ounce of air and attention she possessed. She was too terrified to move, yet here she was sailing across the open field. At that moment, life was an oxymoron for Jo. In those few seconds of flight, she saw the event in a slow motion play that seemed to last forever. Her eyes gazed upon the beauty of the mountains, while her brain alerted her to certain death.

At the end of the thirty second eternity, she landed safely on the other side, caught by Lori and the brake-stop put in place to slow her harness. In another 30 seconds, she was standing on the platform, and had even managed a weak smile.

"Ok, so we didn't die, the cable didn't break, the harness didn't snap, and it was quite a ride - I'll give you that much, Gina. But I haven't soared over a tree top yet, and I still don't feel like assuming the Superman position to get from point A to point B."

"You just can't admit that it was fun, can you?"

"Yes, yes, yes. It was fun," a somewhat breathless and sarcastic Jo exclaimed. "It wasn't as scary as I thought it would be, and I see what you mean about the landing. I never dreamed it would be that easy. Where to next?"

From that point forward, these two women behaved more like school girls than women nearing their sixties. Gina didn't outdo Jo by much on the posing and Jo did eventually try the Superman flying position. Neither were ready for the adventure to be over as they approached one of the final landing platforms.

It had been great. The views were stunning. The cables that stretched from platform to platform gave each zipliner the opportunity to survey the trees and mountains that surrounded them. Lush branches of green extended from tall trees and the floor of the forest was covered with all sorts of ground cover. Green was everywhere around and beneath them. From high atop the platforms, you could view the surrounding mountain tops, framed with the blue of the sky and cream puff clouds. It was a fantastic sight.

"Alright ladies, this will be your last time to zip to a landing platform. After this ride, you'll leave the final platform and land on the ground. No more circus tricks and no more flying through the treetops." Tammy turned to ask which one to buckle, but Jo was already first in line.

"I'm going first this time – Gina's got to go first every other jump – this one's mine."

"Okay Miss Timid, you get to go first. But you need to know one more thing. Since we're not up as high as we have been, you'll need to really push to get yourself across this section. It doesn't have as much fall as the others. That means you have to walk as close to the edge of the platform as possible, lean forward, and push hard with your legs, got it?"

Jo groaned inwardly. *Naturally the one she wanted to go first on was going to be more complicated.*

"I got it – I can do it. Buckle me up."

Tammy attached her carabineer to the cable and waited for Lori's "ready" call. In a few minutes, Lori gave the call.

"Ok, Jo, time to go."

Jo walked to the edge of the platform. Holding onto the harness with a grip of steel, she leaned slightly forward. Instead of being able to catch herself, and wait for a chance to push, she lunged over, and slid off the platform. The harness caught, and she moved forward over the zipline, but not at a great rate of speed.

She enjoyed the view, but wasn't too sure she was going fast enough to reach the other side. As she poised to reach the last platform she ground to a near halt. and Lori extended her hand and grabbed at the harness and cable. She missed. Jo hadn't come in with enough speed for Lori to grab her at just the right moment.

For a split second Jo was motionless. As she drew close enough to reach for Lori's hand, the harness began to slide backwards on the cable.

Oh, dear Lord. I'm sliding backwards, what the hell... I'll be stranded out in the middle if this thing doesn't slow down...

"Oh my gosh, oh my. Jo, I'm so sorry!" Lori bellowed from the platform, realizing the wasted effort of extended hand.

Jo could see Gina waving and laughing from behind her.

It's probably best that I can't hear her... I bet she's having a field day with this...

Jo turned her attention to Lori and did her best to sound convinced that she would be alright.

"What do I do now?" she called from midway between platforms.

"Just sit tight, I'm gonna send out a backpack with a rope attached. I'll have to pull you in."

Sit tight… what else am I gonna do? Undo the harness and free fall? NOT!

Jo looked at the ground beneath her. It really wasn't that high at this point, they were almost at the bottom of the zipline. She probably could've undone her harness and fell to the ground, except for her already bruised ankle. *Well, that idea won't work.*

There was also the fact that touching the carabineer and harness connected to the cable was a no-no. That had been one of their first instructions as they prepared to leave the first platform.

Jo looked back. There was Gina with her phone, camera rolling.

"Gina," she hollered, "I know you're not taking pictures of this."

"No, I'm not. I'm making a video of this!" Gina half-hollered half-giggled back to her.

"No, you're not!"

"Yes, I am – and you're not really in a position to stop me!" Full blown laughter erupted from the platform.

Dear God, there's no telling what she'll do with that video.

A slow several minutes passed as Lori fed the backpack from her platform out to Jo. Jo tried her best to inch herself along in the direction of the pack. Slowly, slowly, the pack neared.

"See if you can grab it Jo, I've sent it as far as I can." Lori called to her from the distance.

"I'm trying, it's still several feet away, let me see if I can push myself forward some more." Jo began to rock her harness. Slowly she moved towards the backpack.

Almost….

"Got it!"

As she grabbed the pack and held on with a steel grip, Lori began to pull her in via the rope attached to the pack.

Inch by inch, foot by foot, she moved closer to the platform.

"Ah, gotcha ya!" Lori exclaimed.

An exhausted Lori finally pulled an elated Jo onto the platform.

"I'm so sorry I didn't catch you – that should never happen. But, it does occasionally. At least you were calm and cool headed. I missed once before when I tried to catch a fairly tall man. By the time I got him, he was on the verge of a panic attack."

"Well, I wasn't going to fall. And, if worst came to worst, I could've released the carabineer and dropped to the ground, so I wasn't that afraid."

Jo surprised herself. *Here she was Miss Scaredy Cat, calm as a cucumber.*

"Alright, let's see if we can get Miss Gina over without making the same mistake twice."

"Oh, you won't. She'll fly off of that platform like a winged bird. She'll have enough speed, catching her won't be an issue."

Sure enough, as Lori shouted over the usual "ready", Gina pushed like a woman possessed and flew right on over.

Jo reached for her phone as she landed, but Gina had tucked it tightly into the front pocket of her jeans.

"Oh, no, missy. I knew you'd try that… that video isn't getting deleted. It's going to get 'shared'."

"C'mon. Let me see it."

"You can when we get back to the jeep. After, I've had time to save it and share it."

Tammy broke into their conversation to thank them for the opportunity to share their adventure and move them along to the last jump, the last "zip" across the forest; this time, they would be landing on the ground.

Jo spotted the ATV waiting as she made her final descent.

"Hey, at least we don't have to walk," and she pointed at the side by side. "We can ride back up the hill."

It was only a few minutes and they were back at the block building, removing their harnesses.

"Gina, you and Jo were great fun – grandmothers are actually some of our best customers."

Grandmothers?? Do I look like a grandmother? Jo was suddenly very aware that even if she didn't *feel* like a grandmother, she might *look* like one.

They turned to thank Tammy and Lori, as well as Julie, who took their harnesses and hung them back in their appointed slots on the wall.

"Ladies, you guys were great guides. I can truthfully say, I wasn't too excited with this idea. Gina was the one that booked the tour. Now that it's over, I'm really glad she did. We had a great time!"

"And we'll be back again!" Gina added. "Maybe this summer!"

Laughing and saying goodbyes, they made their way to the jeep.

"See, I told you this would be fun…"

"Yes, you did. And I've got to say, I was petrified on that first jump; once I realized I wasn't going to plunge to my death, it turned out to be a great experience."

"See, I told you."

"Now, I don't know about you, but I'm starving – ready for lunch? Let's go back to the store, and see what they've got for Sunday dinner, if there's any left, it's almost 1."

Jo cranked the jeep. *Yes, she was hungry too. What great fun that had been. Once again, Gina had pushed her to do something that she discovered she enjoyed… maybe she* was *worth keeping as a friend…*

Just for fun, Jo gunned the jeep, and threw Gina backwards, two could play at that.

CHAPTER 6

But this time, Lord, you gave me a mountain
A mountain you know I may never climb.
It isn't just a hill any longer
You gave me a mountain this time....

Elvis Presley

IN A FEW SHORT minutes, they were pulling up to the front of the store. There were only two other vehicles in the parking lot, but the front porch was full of people.

"Where did all these people come from? There's not hardly any vehicles. How did they get here?"

"They walked, silly. Have you forgotten you're in some of the best walking country in the world?"

"Oh, yeah, I guess I did forget, or it just never occurred to me so many folks were here."

"Well, it's Sunday, and almost everybody that stayed in a cabin has packed up any food; it's just easier to come over here and eat. That way they're ready to go right after lunch."

"Kinda like we were supposed to do?"

"Yeah, but we didn't pack anything this morning – we've still got an afternoon of packing. We might as well eat first. Let's go see what's left."

As they tromped up the short steps to the store, Maxine darted out the doorway.

"I was wonderin' if you were gonna come back by here before ya'll left."

"You know I wasn't leavin' without tellin' you bye."

The two embraced, and Maxine ushered them into the store.

"I saved a little food for you two, I thought you might be hungry after that ziplining excursion, and I was right, uh?"

"Yes ma'm you were, we're starved!"

They took a seat at the first empty table they came to, and Maxine disappeared into the kitchen to retrieve the food she'd saved. When she came back, Max was right behind her.

As Maxine placed the plates on the table, she turned to Jo.

"How's your arm and leg and let's see… was it your ankle?"

"Oh, they're much better today. I haven't even given any thought to my arm and leg. The ankle's been a little sore, but nothing I couldn't handle; even on the zipline."

"Good." It was Max that spoke. "I was hoping you'd be up for a little visit today, and we can talk more about your military experience. It seems you know my son, George."

There was a moment of pointed silence.

Jo was more than a little stunned. In fact, she was downright flabbergasted. Yes, she had thought George might know them, but this couldn't be the crazy parents he referred to in D.C.

"George Durand is your son?" Surprise was clear in the tone of her response.

"Yes, he is. Gina says you worked up there with him in Washington. What'd you do? Same thing he does?"

"Yes," she answered, somewhat hesitantly.

"Mmmm… I see. I suppose George has already told you how we view all that stuff up there in Washington, too, right?"

"Yes," again Jo replied with hesitancy. She hoped this wasn't going in the direction she instinctively thought it was.

"Well, would you like to hear the other side of the story? Or, are you like George, too close minded to consider an old man might possibly be right?"

"Well, no sir, I mean yes sir. I'd like to hear your side of the story, and I'm not so close minded that I'm not willing to listen."

"Well good. Too bad George didn't have enough sense to keep a girl like you. You seem like you've got some common sense, and if you grew up here, you can't be all bad."

Jo's face flamed. She wasn't sure if it was the remark concerning George 'keeping' her, or that she couldn't be all bad.

"You wanna eat first, or talk first?" Max gestured to her plate. The food was untouched.

Maxine stood listening to the exchange. Watching for any sign of an impending explosion. Here was a chance to delay any immediate anger.

"Oh, let the woman eat, Max. You've got all afternoon to talk. Let's go clean up the kitchen, then you can come back and talk to her when she's finished."

Jo wasn't sure if she could eat – her stomach was lurching as though it was full of rocks *and* butterflies.

"When did you tell him I knew George?" Jo demanded as soon as they were out of earshot. "Why didn't you tell me? I could've been a little better prepared."

"I forgot. He told me last night at the fire, but I was having a good time, and honestly, Jo, it slipped my mind."

"How could you forget that?" she almost spat the word out.

"We just got to laughing and talking and visiting with Aunt Mary and…"

"What the hell has Aunt Mary got to do with remembering a conversation?"

This time it was Gina that stared blankly at her friend.

She really doesn't know. She doesn't know what that is. Oh my God, how sheltered can you be?

"Look, I'm sorry I forgot. But I warned you that Max and Maxine were different. That they had a story. Now, it seems, George is part of that story. If you don't want to talk to him, I'll go tell him we don't have time. We can talk next time."

"No, I don't want to not talk to him. I just wish I hadn't been caught so off guard. George means the world to me and he's been a dear, dear friend. He's smart, committed, and he really helped me when I first got to Washington. I don't want them to try to change my opinion."

"Oh, they're not. They're proud of George. Max and Maxine just don't agree with the government on some of the policies that George helps to carry out."

"Here, let's eat, we can talk in a minute. I gotta have some food." As she finished her sentence, she filled her mouth with homemade stew, cornbread, and sweet tea. *Ahhh… the joy of a home cooked meal.*

They sat in silence as they each consumed the plateful of food Maxine had brought them. They finished it off with a bowl of banana pudding she had placed in the middle of the table.

Just as they put down their forks and spoons, and as if on cue, Max and Maxine emerged from the kitchen.

"I bet they were watchin' us eat." Gina giggled. "Waitin' to pounce the minute we were through."

"Dear God, please let this go better than I am certain it's going to," Jo half moaned, half whispered and wholeheartedly prayed.

"Ok, now, let's pick up where we left off… where was I? Oh, yeah.

I want to tell you a little relating to Maxine and myself before I talk to you about George, which by the way, we *are* very proud of our son. It's not his achievements and life that we have a problem with. Anyway, back to me and Maxine."

For the next half hour, Max shared with Jo the particulars surrounding their journey to the mountains. Why he retired from the chemical plant and the dangers many of the chemicals they were producing posed to the environment. He shared with her his own exposure to dangerous levels of something called "methyl bromide", and finally, his discovery of the NSA.

"You ever heard of them? I bet you have, George knows who they are. He doesn't believe they're spying on us, but he's familiar with the division."

"Yes sir, I know the agency you're referring to, but they aren't authorized to spy on the American public. They're in place to protect us against terrorists and terroristic plots, like 9-11."

"Since when do you think this great big government tells you everything they're doin'? You know anything about Tuskegee, Alabama?"

Jo had heard of the experiment performed on the enlisted black men of Tuskegee. She knew the government injected soldiers with syphilis, purposefully and without their knowledge or permission.

"Yes sir, I know."

"Now, do you *really* think they won't spy on you? You better think again. I know for a fact, the last year me and Maxine were in Louisiana, they tapped our phone. They were interested in what I might or might not say when it came to methyl bromide."

"Now, how can you know that? You think you're gonna be able to detect if someone's listening to you?"

"Sure you can. And you can watch and see what's happening around you, too. That's when I decided to investigate the spy agencies of the government. That's when I discovered the NSA, and all their capabilities. I've known for nigh on twelve years now. It's also why we decided to move up here. Get off the grid. Rebel against 'big brother'. And it's worked, too. You don't get many government folks up here, and if you do, it's really hard to find us when they show up."

"But Mr. Durand, the NSA is NOT spying on the American people, I can promise you that's not their mission."

"And I can promise you they *are*. I can't prove it, but they are."

Something tugged at Jo's memory. Something in a line of code she and George had questioned. What was it? What had caught her attention? Jo didn't have the luxury of following the thought. Max's look demanded her attention and an answer. She abandoned the thought almost as quickly as it had come.

"Alright, suppose they are – what do George and I have to do with that? We protect government computer privacy. We protect our military intellectual property from other governments, not anything to do with the NSA."

"It's all intertwined, Jo. You can't separate the good from the bad anymore with that bunch up there in Washington – everybody's greasin' everybody else's palms. Black and white, right and wrong aren't clear lines anymore. It's all a great big gray area. And now, rules and regulations are created based on how much you can extort from somebody or some government. That's my problem with what you and George do: you're unsuspecting enablers of illegal government activity."

"You can't seriously believe that? *Really*? You don't even truly know what we do, or you couldn't possibly say that."

Jo's mind, and her sensibilities reeled from the insinuations Max had made. She wasn't an enabler of anything, especially anything illegal. She, and others like her, made extremely valuable contributions towards protecting the country against piracy and dangerous at-tacks – she had nothing to do with the NSA. Or did she?

As her thoughts played out in her mind, the evidence and reali-zations of those thoughts played out on her face. Max watched as she truly contemplated the results, the true product of the role she and George had played in the world of cyberspace.

"I see a light – a light of greater understanding. Too bad I've never seen that light on George's face. He's too mired in the fact that I'm his old man to seriously contemplate what I'm saying. You're not. You mull over the things we've talked about this afternoon, Jo. We'll have a further discussion at a later date – of that I'm sure."

"Oh, and I also want to leave you with one additional thought. We're a family up here, Jo. A family that sits down and talks. We don't hide behind texts and emails or clicks on a webpage or that legal bunch of mumbo-jumbo double-talk like you get in Washington. If half of those folks were as straight forward as they're supposed to be, we wouldn't be in the damn mess we're in today."

And with those words, Max abruptly stood and excused himself from the conversation. His departure left Jo somewhat irritated and confused.

Was there any truth to Max's statements? Had their work been as he said "an unsuspecting enabler" of the government's efforts to spy on the American people?

As she struggled to recover from the conversation, Gina and Maxine had moved on to another topic: the newest resident of the RV Park.

"Where is this new guy, Paul? I thought you said he was going to be here this summer? I wanted to meet him."

"Well, I'm not sure where he is. You know, he came up here and met Max. I didn't get to meet him, and he told Max he'd be back this summer. He was supposed to bring his camper and take up residence in the Park. Well, you know Max, he can't remember what happened yesterday, much less a few months ago. He doesn't remember the man's last name or where he's from. Anyway, he's interested in buying all these cabins we've got. You know Gina, it's gettin' too much for me and Max. Max did remember that he had some business in California," and she paused. "That's where he's from. So, he called Max and told him it might be late fall before he gets up here. He also told him not to worry, he still wants to talk to him if the cabins are still for sale. I told Max to keep up with the rental income this summer so when they talk this fall he'll know what kind of price to give the man. Will he listen? Who knows."

"Oh, Maxine – you're going to give up the cabins? No! I love coming up here and staying with you guys. Reckon he'll change anything? Will I still be able to get Cabin #2 on a whim, like this weekend?"

"I don't know, Gina honey. It's finally come to the place that we don't need so much to tend to. You'll get there one of these days. And I know Max, he'll make sure this Paul is a good guy. We thought Bob and Lucy might wanna take over some day, but after several conversations, they told us they have other plans."

"Gina," Jo interjected, "we really need to get over to the cabin and get packed. It's almost 3 o'clock. It'll be 4 before we can leave, and I've got a class to teach tomorrow. I've got to get home at a decent hour."

Gina knew there was much more to Jo's desire to go and pack. She could tell by the tone of her voice that there was more conversation to be had while they packed *and* on the way home.

They both said their goodbyes to Maxine, and told her to tell Max as well, as he had not returned to the table after his abrupt departure.

As they climbed into the jeep to make the short drive over to the cabin, Gina wanted to continue their conversation. The thundercloud on Jo's face kept her silent.

CHAPTER 7

She's got a smile that it seems to me
Reminds me of childhood memories...
Where everything was as fresh as the bright blue sky....

Guns-n-Roses

THE PACKING PROCESS WAS a short and silent one. Although both women had things to say, neither was willing to take the leap into a full blown conversation. Not until they were safely seated in the jeep and several miles were between them and their weekend retreat.

It was finally Gina that took the leap.

"Jo, I really am sorry I forgot to mention my discussion with Max about George, but why were you so offended? Sure, Max has a different opinion than you. But he wasn't insulting your work or its importance in your life."

"Yes, he was. Perhaps not intentionally, but he was. I've spent my life committed to government objectives, which by the way, were objectives I embraced as well. Max just threw it back in my face."

"You're looking at this all wrong. You're only thinking of your beliefs and your experience. Didn't you hear Max's story? Can't you stop to see his side?"

"He and Maxine lived a completely different life to yours; with a completely different view of the government. They've watched as it's grown to a size that often disregard's citizens beliefs and traditions. You were in the middle of that environment. You haven't noticed all the changes taking place in small town America. If you want to better understand Max and Maxine, you have to be willing to see life from their perspective."

"Who says I want to get to understand them? Their view is so different from mine. Why would I want to even try to understand their position?"

Gina was silent for a few minutes. She never dreamed Jo would be so offended by Max. She also never thought they would have such different opinions.

I love Max and Maxine. I assumed Jo would too. How have we become so different? We grew up together. How can there be such a divide?

She finally spoke.

"We should lay this aside right now. Let's have a pleasant trip home. After all, we've got a long time to discuss our differences Jo. Let's try to focus first on our similarities. We've been apart for so long; if all we do now is talk and worry over the things that divide us, we'll never rediscover the things that bind us."

Jo sighed. She really wasn't in the mood for further confrontation. Discussing Max and his beliefs would only create further confrontation.

"Fine, we can shelve that for now. I really don't want to ride a couple of hours arguing my side of 'big government interference' anyway."

As she finished her sentence, she reached for a cigarette. It would calm her, whether it was the nicotine or simply the motion, it had a calming effect.

"You find comfort in those don't you? That's one reason you don't give them up. I can understand that. When I had my hysterectomy…"

"You had a hysterectomy? You didn't tell me that, when? Why?"

"Yeah, oh my, it was years ago. Millie was five. Mom had already passed, and I started having real trouble every month. Every time I started, it was horrible. My hormones were going nuts and I'd hurt so bad it would take me several days to recover. Right before I finally had the hysterectomy, I would spend a couple of days a month in the bed."

"Poor Robert, he had no idea what to do. One minute I'd be happy and laughing, and the next pissed off and crying. It went on this way for nearly a year. That was a really, really hard time for me *and* for Robert. We basically quit talking. He didn't want to risk dealing with a crazy wife and I just didn't feel like much of a human being. Even the kids tiptoed around when it was that time of the month."

"What did you do? Didn't you go to the doctor? How'd you figure out you needed a hysterectomy? Especially so young?"

"Yeah, I finally did go to a gynecologist over in Flowood. Robert finally told me I had to go see what was wrong. He truly couldn't take it anymore and I thought I was losing my mind. Something had to give."

"Anyway, it didn't take the gynecologist long to figure out I had something called 'endometriosis' and that it was a pretty bad situation. When they called with the results, they said I needed to come back to the office. The nurse that called also said to bring my husband with me. Hell, I thought I had cancer they sounded so serious."

"Anyway, Robert and I went for the appointment. Once we were called back, they started talking surgery. A hysterectomy because of the endometriosis; Robert looked like he was gonna walk out. It was making him really uncomfortable, I wasn't too sure why though. I mean, we really didn't want any more kids."

"You know, he never did really wanna talk that much about it. Not even after the surgery and finally everything kinda got back to normal. He was that way though. He didn't never talk much when I got pregnant with Jax. And, he didn't ever wanna talk about that time in our life when I was so out of sorts. I never understood why. Because of the accident, I never got a chance to really talk to him. I always thought we'd revisit those years after the kids were grown. I never got the chance."

"Wow. I had no idea. Do you take hormones, now?"

"Oh, yeah. And I learned early on, how important those things are. Not long after the surgery, I'd say somewhere around 6 months, I decided one day I didn't wanna take them anymore. I mean, I felt great, why did I need to take that stuff? Big mistake. The hormones keep you from becoming crazy as hell. I spent a couple of days like some wild maniac. The only thing I didn't do was foam at the mouth!" Gina bubbled with laughter.

"After a couple of days like that, Robert got the medicine out of the cabinet and said 'TAKE IT – NOW'."

Gina bubbled with laughter at this point.

"I haven't missed a day since."

"Dear God, Gina how awful. I can't imagine! I've been going through menopause myself for a couple of years now, but my biggest problem is the night sweats. The doc put me on a little pill, and for the most part, I don't have them anymore. Only every once in a while."

"It was pretty awful. The worst part was Robert's distance. We really had a rough time in our relationship. I felt like he avoided me and, to a certain extent, he did. He'd work late. Much later than before, and on weekends if he could find somebody to fish or hunt with, he was out the door. Once again, I had to deal with an issue all alone."

"I really hate that we were so far apart during all this. I guess it couldn't be helped, we were at such different places in our lives."

"I know. Melvin tried to help me through all that. When I had errands to run, I used to stop by the Krusty Kupp. Melvin was like a bartender, only all he served up was coffee, or at least that's what I thought."

"I stopped by there one morning, before I had the hysterectomy and I was a mess. I guess I really did look kinda nuts. Anyway, Melvin brought me a cup of coffee and sat down at the table with me. He asked how things were going and all of sudden I burst out crying. I never saw it coming and I know poor Melvin didn't. As we finished the conversation, he slid his hand over to pat mine and slipped me a joint. I'll never forget what he said. 'Gina, take this and go home. Maybe it'll mellow things out for you, for a little while anyway.'"

"You took it? Seriously? You smoked it?"

"I sure did. And he was right. I got better that day and several more." She laughed rather nervously.

Might as well go ahead and tell her now. So much for avoiding more confrontation and finding similarities.

"I still smoke occasionally. I can tell by the look on your face, you're not too happy with that either. Right?"

"It's illegal! You realize that don't you? Pot IS illegal!"

Once again, Jo's senses reeled from Gina's revelation. *My God, what's happening? Have I totally and completely entered a warp zone this weekend?*

"I know it's illegal, but have you ever stopped to think how many things were once illegal that we do every day now? Remember, alcohol and prohibition? And besides, pot wasn't always illegal. Henry Ford wanted to make cars out of it at one point in time."

Alarm bells were ringing in Jo's head.

This cannot be happening. She didn't just tell me that. Who is this person?

"Ah, now I see. This is what you were speaking of on the way up here. Doin'g things that are not so 'socially acceptable'. I had no idea it would be that though. How can you think it's ok? Because in your opinion it's not such a 'bad' drug? It's still illegal, Gina. And by the way, Henry Ford wanted to make cars out of 'hemp', not pot."

"Well, I don't think it will always be. Some states are trying to legalize it now. It doesn't make sense to keep fighting a losing battle."

"Who says it's a losing battle? What did you get that information? Have you checked the stats on drug consumption in this country?"

"Are you forgetting I've spent over a decade dealing with drug rehab? Of course I know statistical information. And I can tell you this, we're losing the war on drugs, not winning. Look at all the drugs that are smuggled across our borders. Drugs like pot, cocaine and heroin flow into this country like running water every day. Never mind the dangers of the drug cartels themselves and the chaos on our borders because of it. We've got much bigger problems in this country to solve than worrying over who's smoking a joint. And besides, what if cigarettes were illegal tomorrow? Would you stop smoking immediately just because of legality?"

Gina was quite incensed when she finished her sentence.

Such hypocrisy. Here she is addicted to a legal drug, and she wants to preach to me.

She could also tell Jo wasn't going to capitulate on her position.

Well, here we are, at odds again.

A deafening silence fell between them.

Not even the beauty of the Ozarks could draw them into a conversation at that moment.

For almost thirty minutes they rode in silence. Each with their own thoughts.

Finally, the ding of Jo's phone broke the silence.

"It's George. I haven't talked to him since his dilemma on Friday. Are you ready to stop for a minute? I'll answer him, we can take a bathroom break and get a snack."

"Sure, pull over at the next chance. I'm ready to get out and stretch my legs anyway. What dilemma? You still help him, even now, from home?"

"Yes, it's primarily because we're such close friends. Things I worked on were different versus George's abilities. Maggie took my place, but apparently they still need my input. I'll give him a shout while we're stopped."

"You've not told me much when it comes to Maggie and George. When we finish our break, would you mind telling me a little more? I'd like to get to know some of your friends, like I wanted you to meet mine. Even if I can only get to know them through our conversations."

"Actually, I'm hoping they can come for a visit around Labor Day. I want you to meet them while they're here. *And,* you can see for yourself why I had such a hard time with Max's comments."

It was only a few short miles before Jo saw the opportunity to stop. There was a Texaco sign pointing the way.

As she brought the jeep to a stop in the parking lot, Gina grabbed her purse.

"You want anything while I'm in there?"

"No, I'm coming in a minute. It won't take but a second to talk to George, then I'll take a bathroom break and grab a bag of chips."

Jo picked up her phone and hit the button labeled "George". It only took two rings for George's familiar "Jo!" on the other end.

"Hey, George. How's it going? Crazy weekend! But you first, what's up?"

"I need to know something. There is an issue with some code you wrote for the interface between the DOD and the NSA's systems. You actually might need to be in front of your computer. Where are you? What happened this weekend? I thought you were going hiking on some mountain? What happened, a bear chase you?" He followed his sentence with a snicker that she was meant to hear.

"Well, yes we did cross paths with a bear, but that's not the big news; guess who I met in those mountains?"

"Uh, your old flame, what's his name, Paul something or other?"

"No, nobody from my youth. These folks were from your youth."

"Who in the hell could you meet in the Ozark Mountains of Arkansas from my youth? I grew up in Louisiana."

"Apparently, you are directionally challenged George. Your parents don't live in Missouri; they live in Arkansas."

"Oh, dear Lord! You didn't? Seriously? Crazy and crazier live in the mountains you went to hike? Tell me you didn't meet them, say it ain't so!"

"Oh, yes I did. I did most definitely meet them. And, might I add that your father is quite the opinionated individual. It only took five minutes for us to be at odds with each other over the government and the work we do."

"Oh, I can only imagine how that conversation went down. I'm so sorry, Jo. I really thought their place was in Missouri. All the mail I get comes from a Missouri address, not Arkansas. Oh God, I never dreamed this would happen." Amidst his feigned horror, Jo could hear the laughter in his voice. "I can't wait to hear all this." The laughter rolled out at that point, no longer a hint, but a full blown cackle.

"Well, it'll have to wait. I'm still with Gina, and she thinks the world of them. I'll call you back as soon as I get home, should only be an hour or so, at most. We'll share computer time while we discuss the radical views of the mysterious Max and Maxine."

"Oh yeah. That will be a conversation for the record books. Ok, talk to you then. I'm gonna need a little while to absorb this news anyway."

As they hung up, Gina was coming out the door of the store, chips and drink in hand.

"Ok, your turn. I'll sit with the jeep."

Jo was only gone for a few minutes. When she got back to the jeep, Gina was behind the wheel.

"My turn to drive. You shouldn't have to do all the heavy lifting, we can share the job. Hop in."

As they pulled out of the parking lot, Jo opened her chips and soda and Gina finished hers.

"Ok, now, tell me about George and Maggie."

CHAPTER 8

And I think it's gonna be a long long time..
Til touchdown brings me round again….

Elton John

"WELL, I GUESS I'LL start at the beginning. You already know I met Maggie at the Academy. Her name then was Margaret Ann Wilson, and she is from Muscle Shoals, AL. We were both country come to town then, but I guess Maggie was a little more street smart than myself. And in a way, she reminded me of you. At any rate, we bunked together and hit it off right from the start. We went through the Academy, and then we served together several times during our commissions. Maggie has such a horse-sense approach to life and she's been a close friend for years. We've always talked. Sometimes we laughed… and sometimes we cried."

"She was with me in France, and then in Japan. Only she didn't get to Japan until I was almost finished. When she did show up, she had a husband. Never called to tell me, never even hinted at the fact in our phone conversations. But that's Maggie. She won't even tell you she's contemplating something – until boom – it happens."

"Anyway, she married her third cousin on her momma's side, a guy named James Johnson, aka 'Jimmy'. When she retired in '96, she moved back home to Muscle Shoals. I still think Maggie married him mostly because she was lonely. I do think she loved him, but when he passed away, she wasn't the devastated grieving widow. Within two weeks she was in Washington looking for a job."

"You're kiddin'? She was ready to go to work in two weeks? Jo, I was a heapin' hot mess for months after Robert died. Two weeks, really?"

"Well, like I said, Maggie's a different one. She showed up in Washington one day. Hell, I didn't even know Jimmy had died, much less that she was coming and she's been there ever since."

"She said she had to get out of Muscle Shoals, 'cause everybody was driving her crazy, cryin' and moanin' over Jimmy dyin, but I know better. Maggie wanted to get out of Muscle Shoals because she missed her work and with Jimmy gone, she was once again alone."

"Well, did she do the same thing as you in the military or just since she got to Washington?"

"Yeah, Maggie trained on most of the same things I did at the Academy. In fact, we shared a lot of classes, a lot of cigarettes, and a lot of confidences. Now, when she got to Washington, I gave her a crash course in upgraded information, especially since she had been out of the loop for so long. A lot had changed since she retired. She still can't do all of the things I did, hence the reason George still calls."

"Oh yeah, now for George and his parents. Is he anything like them at all? When Lucas, their oldest son came to see them last year I discovered he's a lot like Maxine: quick and a real people-person. What about George?"

"Hmmm… no, I can't say that George would remind you of either of his parents. He's not a people person, that's for sure. He'd rather be hidden in a room full of computers than to be chatting with even one customer in a mountain store . He looks like your typical geek, bald and glasses. He's about the same height as Max and slender like Maxine, but that's as far as it goes."

"And, how did you say you met George?"

"We met initially in Germany, early on in our careers; then we seemed to go in completely separate directions. He wasn't a close friend until Edwards Air Force base in California. When we worked together there, we really became close. After that, we kept in touch and even had a chance to visit with each other a couple times on assignments."

"But you two never dated? How strange, you have so much in common."

"That we do, but George and I never felt that way about each other. We really, really just enjoyed each other's company - nothing more, nothing less."

"We used to spend lots of nights after work at a local hangout in D.C. That's when George would tell me about his parents. They came to visit George a couple of times while I was there, but he was very careful to keep his distance from me and work when they came. It wasn't that he was 'secretive'. I truly think he was scared to death about what they might say or do if he wasn't around. As this weekend as proven, I don't think George thought we would see eye to eye. Anyway, they rarely stayed over a couple of days and then George would have another round of stories to tell. He could always make us laugh as we shared a round of drinks. Yes, he could tell quite the stories."

"Mmm… I see. No wonder you were so shocked when you learned they were his parents. They're nothing alike. I can't get over the fact that they have a son that works at the Department of Defense. Those two would make great extras in a Wild West show, not a James Bond movie."

"That goes to prove once again, you can't judge a book by its cover. You certainly can't judge the kids by looking at their parents."

"No, you can't, and that brings me to my next observation. I know so many people who don't have children. What does that say about me? There's you, Melvin, and now George. And, oh yeah, does Maggie have any kids?"

"No, she didn't marry until it was too late for that. She's like me, she'll grow old without anybody to see about her. We'll probably find a nursing home and share a room. If I know Maggie, it'll be required to have a bar and a bingo hall! Beyond that, she won't care!"

They both laughed at the image of two old women in a bar in a nursing home.

"Looks like you're the only one that managed to follow a more traditional path. At least you have children and grandchildren. And that brings *me* to a question: didn't you say Millie worked in the Buffalo River area?"

"Yes, she does. She's a Park Ranger. She normally stays somewhere around the Hemmed In Hollow trail. We just didn't make it over her way this time. Maybe the next time we go, we could hike that trail and stay in one of the little cabins that the National Park maintains. They're not quite as nice as Max and Maxine's, but they're ok."

"Next time?"

"Yeah, surely you want to go again? We've had the best time ziplining and hiking. You used to love these mountains, and I figured we'd go again in a couple of weeks. Perhaps Melvin can go the next trip if I can pull him out of that diner."

"Oh, and what about Melvin? Exactly what kind of relationship do you two have? You hardly ever do anything together. In fact, you've not even mentioned him this weekend."

"Melvin is complicated, Jo. We really care for each other. It's just that he seems to already be married to a business. When we first began to date, if you wanna call it that, I thought it would be like when I dated Robert. I know that was a lot of years ago and I was a teenager then; but still, dating is dating. Right? Wrong. Melvin's idea of a relationship is quite different from mine."

"If he's not working, or if he's not working on something at work, then he'll make time for me. He's really not that interested in hiking or family events. He hardly ever comes to dinner at Thanksgiving or Christmas or any of the grandkids birthdays. It's really hard to have a relationship with someone who's never around."

Jo had a puzzled expression on her face, then she turned to Gina.

"He's not so different from myself. All those years in the military, I never made time for anything much beyond work. Most of my friends were also coworkers. Have we become a generation of work-a-holics? Is that all we've done with our lives? Just work, work, work? No time for families, or husbands and wives, never mind pursuing a passion or a hobby?"

Gina was rather quiet.

And I thought I was the different one. At least I had the time for children, family, and making friends from different places, with different views.

"Well, I guess we each make our own choices, Jo. Then we live with them and sometimes we can only make the best of them. That's something I've been doin'g for years, living with my choices, and realizing there was a way to find something good out of the worst of situations. I guess that's also why I wanted to see if we could pick up the pieces. We had a great friendship at one time and I was hoping it could be again. Now that I have time and you have time. Even if we have a few differences to overcome."

It was Jo's turn for contemplation.

A few differences would be an understatement. But they did have moments when it seemed as if no time at all had passed. She was the same person Jo remembered.

"I guess there's a smidgen of truth there. We're grown women now, not teenagers, and there's a lot of distance to cover. We have some really different views, Gina."

"Yeah, I know we do. But what kind of friends would we be if we didn't at least try?"

Jo didn't want to delve any further into something that she needed time alone to sort through. So she simply returned to the conversation about Melvin.

"So why do you and Melvin keep seeing each other if you never do things together? Isn't that the point of a relationship?"

"Well, Melvin and I see each other when it's convenient for Melvin mostly. We rarely go out, he generally comes over after he gets off work. Sometimes he spends the night, sometimes he goes home. I kinda go with the flow. But to answer a question you posed earlier this weekend, I don't think I'll ever want to be 'Mrs. Kroon'. The life Melvin lives is not something I want to try on a permanent, long-term basis."

"So you just see each other for… sex?"

"Yeah, I guess when you get right down to it, there's not much else. Oh, don't get me wrong, Melvin's been a great friend and confidant. He's given me great advice and helped me through some really rough spots. But I don't think we have a future together. If I'm gonna be alone most of the time, I'd just as soon BE alone. Ya know?"

"That's a really strange relationship Gina. I guess I'm lucky that I haven't ever really tried."

"I would've like to have known what it was like, though. Marriage and kids, having a home, not simply a house. It's too late now, though. This ole body is way past any thoughts of babies!"

Gina laughed. "I don't know Jo, I know some women that are still havin' kids in their late forties. I don't guess 50 plus is out of the question."

"It is at the Felsenthal household. If I thought I had to have a baby right now, I'd just as soon shoot myself in the head, than listen to a crying, squalling baby. Noooo… not yours truly. Not now."

"Well, I truly hate you're gonna miss the grandkids part of the equation. I can't make you understand how much fun grandkids are. You aren't responsible for them: you get to play with'em, spoil'em, and then send them home. And they accept you and love you so much! Bella Kate and Henley Jane are the most precious things I've ever known. In fact, they're absolutely perfect!" As she finished her sentenced she laughed with just the slightest touch of a smirk, "that is, according to 'Ginny', not their mom and dad."

Jo smiled. No, she would never know that. But then she realized, as did Gina, there were a few things they would never share. They were also at the end of sharing a ride. Gina was turning down Jo's drive.

"Good heavens, we're already home. I didn't realize how close we were getting."

"We've been too busy yackin' to notice anything else. I don't know about you, but I'm kinda glad to be back. Nothing or nowhere is as comforting as home."

"You want me to help you load your bags in the car?"

"Naw, I only brought two. I can get'em. I know one thing: I'm lookin' forward to sleepin' in my bed tonight."

"Yeah, me too. And smokin' on my own back porch!" Jo laughed as she threw the comment in to the conversation. She already knew what Gina thought.

Gina confirmed it when she wrinkled her nose and frowned. "You've got a nasty, nasty habit there, Miss Felsenthal."

CHAPTER 9

Well I know it wasn't you who held me down
Heaven knows it wasn't you who set me free
So often times it happens that we live our life in chains
And we never even know we have the key...

Eagles

JO LOCKED THE JEEP as Gina removed her bags. She could wait til in the morning to unpack, there wasn't any hurry and she really didn't feel like unpacking anything this afternoon.

"Jo, thanks for going this weekend. I know it's been a bit of a bumpy ride and I know we have a few differences of opinion. But all in all, it almost seemed like time had never passed – that we hadn't spent so many years apart."

"I know, and I really did have a good time. Except for rolling off the side of the mountain and my meetings with Max."

"Well, you have to learn to take Max in small doses. He's brutally honest about what he thinks, and sometimes it's not what everyone else might think. Just give him a little time. Maybe the next time we go, it'll be a little smoother for you and him."

"We should let my ankle have a few weeks to heal before we strike out again." Jo really wanted to put some time between herself and Max Durand. She wasn't quite ready for anymore of his company.

"Yeah, of course. I was thinking possibly around the 4th of July. There's not quite as much activity on the trails, and we could try Hemmed In Hollow the next time. Besides, Millie would love to see you, and you might get to meet her husband as well. They usually spend the 4th camping with the girls in the National Park. You know, work and play sometimes go hand in hand."

"Ok, yeah, that'll give me a few weeks to heal, and I won't have to rush back to teach a class. We're out that whole week for the holiday. The summer schedule is cramped; although classes are shorter, you still have the same amount of material and as much to try to teach. I haven't decided if I'm going to sign up for a summer class because of the constricted time frame."

Gina laughed. "It's still hard for me to imagine you as a teacher, Jo. You really never seemed to be the type."

"I don't think I could be an elementary or high school teacher, but online isn't so bad. You have to remember, these are college students and I'm not sitting in a class room with them all day, every day."

"That's true. They're a little more interested in learning by the time they get to college and some of your students are really middle-aged adults. I suppose that would make a tremendous difference in your student-teacher relationship. Alright, I'm all loaded up, I need to get home as well. I have a patient to counsel at the clinic tomorrow and I need to check on the grandkids, and Melvin. Not that he will have missed me much, he's probably been at that diner all weekend."

"You wanna get together Thursday morning for coffee?"

"Sure, say around 9? I'll give you a ring on Wednesday to make sure nothing's happened between now and then. Thanks, again, Jo. I really enjoyed it."

With that, Gina hopped in the car and was gone.

Jo was slightly relieved to watch her depart. She enjoyed Gina's company, but so many years of living alone had taught her to enjoy her own company. At the moment, time alone was preferable.

As she unlocked the door to her own cabin, the smell and the surroundings were comforting.

Ah, finally home. Silence, a hot bath and a stint on the back porch. That's what I need; that and time to think.

Jo had never been so confused about a friendship in all her life. There were moments with Gina when she felt like they'd never been apart. And then there were just as many times when she felt like she didn't even know the woman that had ridden beside her all the way home.

She had so many questions swirling around in her head, questions that she didn't want to contemplate right this moment. There would be time for that over the next several days and weeks. Plenty of time to sort things out…

She threw her purse and keys on the counter and headed for the bathroom. First a hot bath, then supper and then the back porch.

Oh, crap. George.

Jo went over the computer and fired it up.

Where's my phone? Surely this won't take long.

She dialed George and waited for him to answer as the computer finished booting.

"Hey, my friend, 'my verbally abused and now shookup' friend. I wasn't sure you'd even call back, at least not today."

"I probably wouldn't if it weren't for the code information you need. To be truthful, I really just want a hot bath, some wine, and time alone."

There was laughter in her voice, and George was quick to steer the conversation towards the code he needed, and away from the family questions he didn't.

"Well, about that code, here's what I need to know…"

They spent the next half hour sorting through lines of code from the executable file Jo had written as an interface between the agencies. George gave her remote access on the secure DOD line, and with just a little investigation, Jo located the problem.

"George, I really don't want to get into all the issues surrounding my conversation with your Dad today, I really am tired. How bout I give you a call Wednesday night. I'll have time to rest and think and let some of the rough edges wear away."

"Sure, that'll be fine. Maggie will probably be around as well, and we can all have a nice chat. We really do miss you here, Jo. Not only for work, either."

"I know, I miss you guys, too. I'll talk to you Wednesday. Bye, George."

Jo's alarm sounded at exactly 5:30am. Not that she needed it this particular morning; she had spent a rather restless night. Between the bruises on her arm, leg, and ankle, not to mention a really overactive mind, sleep had been hard to come by.

Not only had she contemplated her weekend with Gina, she hadn't been able to shake things Max had said during their brief conversation. And she still had this niggling issue with his reference to the NSA and their spying on the American public. There was something, something, she had seen. Something that didn't really make any sense at the time. Now she just couldn't seem to recapture the details from several years and computers screens ago.

How can life just turn completely upside down, without you even realizing its coming? Doesn't this ever stop? When do I get to retire, relax and forget about the military, the DOD, friendship issues and just sit on the porch, drink coffee and read? When?

Thinking of coffee, she got up to go pop a pod in her coffee maker. She did so love her little coffee maker. One cup at a time, any kind you wanted. There were aspects of progress that Jo really loved. Her individual cup of coffee was one.

As it brewed, she got her cigarettes and her phone and waited for the last 'plop' of coffee to drop into her cup. Now, to the back porch and her daily appointment book. Time to think about the responsibilities of Monday.

As she picked up the phone to call her mom, she saw that she had a voicemail.

Mmmm… that wasn't there last night…

She pressed the button to retrieve her voice messages and was startled to hear Paul Collections' voice on the other end.

How strange that he should pick this weekend to call.

"Jo, this is Paul. I really meant to be back home before the summer, but it doesn't look like I'll be finished here. Umm... I guess I just wanted to give you a call, make sure everything was working out with the cabin. And… uh… well, give me a shout if you need anything. My number is 870-911-1313, I sent it in an email, but just in case… anyway, give me a call if you need anything. Talk with you soon."

Well, just when you thought it couldn't get any more complicated.

Now, exactly why did he call? He could've let the office check on me and the cabin.

He'd already given her his cell in the earlier email – and of course it was saved in her inbox.

Later. I'll think about that later. My "later" plate is overflowing.

For the next couple of hours, Jo enjoyed her coffee, called her mom, and planned her lesson for the class. This semester's classes were almost over, and Jo still wasn't sure she was going to sign up to teach a summer class. If her life got any more complicated, she wouldn't have time to teach anything.

The class started at 1 o'clock every Monday and Thursday. Thanks to her life experience, as well as her education, Jo really didn't have any trouble preparing for or teaching her online students. It wasn't that different from what she'd spent the last ten years working on. Too many years in the military as a commissioned officer had eradicated any issues she had with giving instruction. That too, came easily.

She spent the rest of the morning tidying the small cabin, unpacking from her weekend, and trying not to think about the questions that bombarded her mind.

Class lasted only an hour and a half. By 4 o'clock, she'd answered all her student's emails; wrapped up the grading of their weekend assignment and was ready to call it a day. At that moment, her cell phone rang.

"Jo, do you think you could run over here and help me get something out of the attic? I thought of something I needed to give you this weekend, but I can't get it myself."

"Hey, mom. Sure. I just finished my classwork and really don't have anything else I need to do. I'll be there in about a half hour."

She did need to check on her anyway. She'd been gone all weekend, and when she talked to Maureen this morning, she'd said that Stella hadn't been able to come Saturday. There would be things to see about when she got there.

Although her mom was healing physically, there were still gaps in what she could do. Cleaning kitchens and bathrooms were two of those things.

That's why Stella was supposed to come. I really have got to have a talk with her.

Jo was at her mom's in less than a half hour and already deep in conversation and cleaning, when she remembered what Maureen had said when she called.

"Mom, what did you want me to get out of the attic?"

"Oh, yeah. That was why I called. When you get to the top of the stairs, there's a cardboard box way over to the left. It's got

'LETTERS' wrote on it in black magic marker. Get that box and bring it downstairs."

Jo climbed the dusty, dimly lit steps to the attic door. It looked as though there hadn't been anybody up here in years. The attic door wasn't locked, and she swung it open with little effort.

At least it's not rusty or jammed.

As she flipped on the light switch, her eyes adjusted to the dim light and she could see that clutter covered the whole room. Instead of one cardboard box there were at least twenty, scattered in every direction.

Poor Mom. She's forgotten what a mess it is up here...let's see...a box marked LETTERS...

Jo poked around for about fifteen minutes and finally located the box Maureen wanted. It looked like it was about to fall apart and you could barely see the lettering underneath the dust. Jo picked it up carefully and went back downstairs.

"I found it. But it doesn't look like it's gonna hold together much longer – have you got another plastic bin we can put this stuff in? What's in it, anyway?"

"Those are all the letters you wrote to your Dad, Jo. Every single one of them is in that box. He saved them all, and when he passed, I put them in the attic. I've been waiting for the day I could pass them on to you. So, there they are, honey. Your Daddy kept them safe and sound, waiting on you."

There were tears in Maureen's eyes as she thought about Tom. Although it had been years since his passing, there was never a day she didn't miss him. Looking at the letters just brought fresh sorrow to her heart and her eyes.

"Oh, Momma." Jo too, was on the verge of tears. She hadn't thought about the letters in years. She never dreamed her Dad kept any of them, much less all of them.

"He wanted you to have them and would have given them to you himself if circumstances had been different. I wanted to wait til you came home. Really home and until you finally had a permanent place to put them. So, now they're yours."

"You know Jo, me and your Daddy loved both you girls. But your Daddy always had a special soft spot for you, thought you hung the moon. He missed you somethin' fierce when you left. The co-op was never the same for him once you were gone. He still loved his job, don't get me wrong, but the magic of going with you… well, that was over. Those letters lit him up every time one came in the mail. He'd read it again and again, finding something new to tell me every time."

Jo couldn't stop the flow of tears at this point. She wasn't sure if it was the thought of her Dad, the overwhelming weekend, the lonesomeness they each shared or possibly all of it. She and Maureen shared a good cry for several minutes.

Then, as if a light switch went off, Maureen seemed to move on. Her next sentence was about the mess in the kitchen.

Jo was caught completely off guard, once again, by the turn in the conversation and she wondered what was happening in her Mother's head.

Something is not quite right with Mom. I just don't know what.

She let it go and moved on to begin to clean the kitchen and share small talk with Maureen who had followed and was seated at the kitchen table. It took Jo only a few minutes to wash the dishes and tidy the kitchen.

"Alright, Mom. Everything's in order. Did Stella say why she didn't come this weekend?"

"Yeah, when she called Saturday morning, or possibly it was Friday morning she said Hagen had a ball tournament. She'd forgotten about it, and it started at 9 that morning and she didn't know what time she'd be finished."

"Well, couldn't she have come Sunday?"

"No, you know they have church on Sunday, Jo. She couldn't come all the way down here after that. She wouldn't get back home til after dark."

Jo smiled to herself. Maureen had reached the age of planning everything around daylight hours. No travelling after dark, and as a result, everyone else had to be on the same schedule.

"Alright, Momma. I've gotta go now, but I'll be back on Wednesday. Do you need anything from town that I can bring then or do you need me to get you anything now?"

"No, I'm fine. I've got everything I need. I'll be fine til Wednesday. You be careful going home, it's nearly dark out there now."

"I will – love ya Mom. Bye."

Jo's emotions were raw. Between the letters and the events of the past couple of days, she really didn't need to see or talk to anyone tomorrow. Tomorrow was for thinking.

Thinking and cleaning. Cleaning was therapy for Jo, and although she didn't really care for it otherwise, it became a passion when she needed to sort through something in her mind. At times like that, she cleaned with the zeal of a mad woman.

And when Wednesday dawned, the little cabin was the cleanest it had been since Jo's arrival. Too bad her head was not.

By Wednesday afternoon, Jo was no closer to answering her questions than she had been on Monday. She knew Gina would give her a call and although she was no closer to reconciling their differences, she looked forward to their coffee date. She really did enjoy Gina's company.

Jo had barely sat down to the computer to work on Thursday's class, when her cell phone rang. "Gina" was in bold letters on the screen.

"Hey. Calling to remind me?"

"Yes and to make sure nothing has happened to prevent you from coming. Are we still good? Nine in the morning, Krusty Kupp?"

"Yep, we're still good. I'll see you there. I need to talk to you about Mom, anyway. We had the strangest visit Monday, and then when I went to see her today, she didn't even remember giving me the letters."

"What letters?"

"The letters I wrote to Dad when I was overseas. He kept them all and she had stored them in the attic. We even had a good cry on Monday. When I told her I'd read a couple today, she didn't even remember giving them to me. I'm truly at a loss, as to what's going on with her, Gina."

"Well, I'll do a little research, Jo. Perhaps it's a side effect of the surgery, or maybe it's something else. Give me a little time to gather information, then we'll talk about it. See ya!"

As they hung up, the few minutes Jo had spent talking to her improved her mood. It was like talking to Stella, only without the irritation she often experienced when she talked with her older sister.

Lord, help me sort through all this. Too bad I don't still have the base chaplain to go and talk to. And I haven't taken the time to find a church since I've been back. It would really help to have someone to confide in, someone who's not so involved in my situation. Someone that can give me an unbiased point of view. I can't call George. I can't call Maggie, she's too close to George. And although I need to talk to Gina, I need time to sort some of this out with someone else before I talk with her. Dammit, I need…. what do I need? Paul! There's so much time and distance between he and Gina. He doesn't even know Max and Maxine and he won't have a biased opinion because he doesn't know George, either.

She stopped in mid-thought.

Have you lost your mind? Paul doesn't have time for your relation-ship issues. He's a businessman, with business concerns. How would you even begin to start that conversation? Hey, Paul…. listen I just needed a stranger to talk to about my more complicated relationship issues… yeah, right Jo. He'll hop right on that.

But the more she thought about it, the more reasonable it sounded.

Well, you've managed to rationalize this crazy idea to the point of actually calling. Go ahead… what have you got to lose? A place to live? She laughed to herself. *What the hell. Call.*

The sun was already low in the sky Wednesday afternoon before Jo finally mustered the courage to call. And even as she dialed the number, she hadn't really decided how to start the conversation.

This is so out of character for me. I usually know what I want to say and how I want to say it before I ever even begin the conversation. Yet, here I am, willy nilly, placing a call.

She punched the "Paul" button and waited for the phone to ring.

It rang several times and just as she was about to hang up, Paul's "hello" came across the air waves.

Jo was more than a little hesitant. *Fine time to hesitate.*

"Paul, this is Jo. Did I catch you at a bad time?" *Please say yes. This was so such a bad idea.*

"Hey, Jo. No, not really. I'm sort of in between issues and have a few minutes. How are you?"

"I'm fine. I… uh… I just wanted to return your call from Sunday."

"Oh, yeah. I wanted to make sure everything was alright with the cabin. I really thought I would be home before now and have a chance to visit with you. But, things got a little more complicated here than I anticipated. Now it looks like it'll actually be September before I get back."

As Jo was about to reply, Paul interrupted.

"Jo, I'm sorry… I have to take this call. I didn't expect such a quick response from my attorney. Uh, listen, do you have some time later tonight? Can I give you a call back around 5? That'll be about 8 your time."

"Sure, that'll be fine. No worries, I just wanted to return your call. We can talk later."

"Alright, I'll call you at 8. Bye."

"Bye, Paul."

Obviously, God looks out for children and idiots. This time, he saved me from myself.

Jo breathed a long sigh. It had seemed like such a great idea this morning. Right now, however, she was having serious second thoughts.

I don't need to dump this on him. He doesn't have time for my silly issues. I need to sort this out on my own. This is not 1976.

She sat down at the table and picked up the journal she was working on for the year.

Maybe writing it down will help me to see more clearly.

As she wrote, she talked to the journal as if it were a person. She stopped to reflect, talking aloud at times. Sometimes that helped as well. At the end of her writing, she had a list of questions, questions she hoped that in the next few days and weeks she could answer.

As she looked at the pages of her journal she re-read her questions. Suddenly she realized she was at a definite cross-roads in her life.

She looked them over once again:

Really, how much of one's principle's should be sacrificed in the name of friendship?

How much of what I am depends upon my relationship with Gina?

But, how much of what I was at one time, depended on the Gina I once knew?

How much do you owe an old friendship?

How much of my future depends on a friendship with Gina?

Until that Facebook request, I hadn't even given much thought to Gina – why is it so important now?

How can you truly understand the ties that bind? How much does the future depend on the past? And, why does it even matter?

What Jo didn't realize, but soon would, is that these aren't easy questions to answer. How much of our past colors our present, and influences our future? And why does it at some point suddenly seem to matter?

She was so deep in thought, that the ringing of her phone, startled her and made her jump. *Dammit.*

As she reached to answer the phone, she saw that it was Paul.

Was it 8 already?

"Hey, gosh, I didn't even realize it was already 8. I hope I'm not interfering with your schedule, Paul. Really, anything I wanted can wait..."

"No, you're not interfering. I really didn't expect to be interrupted this afternoon when you called. But it's just as well, calling you back now I know there'll be no interruptions. My day is done. Time for a glass of wine, a good meal, and a little time to relax, and talk to an old friend."

They spent the next two hours on the phone. After they shared a long distance glass of wine, Jo wasn't quite so reluctant to share with Paul the real reason for her call.

Somehow, two hours and lots of conversation later, she actually began to sort through her questions; thanks to a little help from an old friend.

Jo was about to turn out the lights and slide slowly into a deep sleep when the phone rang again. She looked down to see "GEORGE" lit up on the translucent screen.

Crap! I forgot.

"Hey, George. Nothing like a *real* friend to forget to call!"

"Yeah. I noticed I'm falling lower and lower on your ladder of importance, Jo. Maggie's noticing it too. What are you doin' out there? Integrating with the locals? Forgetting about us crime-fighters down here in the trenches?"

Although he was joking, Jo felt a pang of guilt. She had moved them down a notch in her life. Even if it was an unintended consequence of her life changes.

"No, I'm not forgetting about you two. I did forget about you tonight. What the heck are you doin' up so late? Why didn't you call earlier? You know that friendship thing is a two-way street. YOU can call ME!"

"Well, to tell you the truth, Jo, I'm never in a real big hurry to talk about my mom and dad. I wouldn't have called now, except Maggie just wouldn't hush. She's insistent when it comes to you. Here, talk to her first."

With that, George handed the phone over and Maggie's no-nonsense southern voice crackled through the speaker.

"Well, you are still alive and well. I'd like to hear all about your meeting with George's parents and how the 'call of the wild' weekend went."

"Yes, I figured you would. You would really enjoy this story! It would so remind you of Alabama! But it's 10 o'clock, and I really, really, am ready for some shut eye. I PROMISE I will call you guys tomorrow night. 8pm sharp, if you'll forgive me this time!"

Jo's voice was cajoling and pleading at the same time. Guilt from the fact that she forgot them along with the effects of several glasses of wine had served to soften her tone and dull her senses. She really, really, only wanted to go to sleep.

"Fine, Miss Felsenthal. But if you forget us tomorrow, I'm coming to wherever it is you are. Where is it now? Deep Shit, Arkansas? No, that's where you'll be tomorrow if you forget us again." Although Maggie laughed as she admonished Jo, she really had been kinda worried.

"Yes, ma'm. I give you my word. I will phone tomorrow night. Now, I'm off to bed. Good-night you two mother hens."

CHAPTER 10

Just remember this, my girl, when you look up in the sky
You can see the stars and still not see the light…

Eagles

GINA CRANKED THE CAR and pulled out of the circle drive.

She smiled as she thought about the last couple of days.

That was truly a lot of fun. I enjoyed time with Jo. There were moments when I felt like it was only yesterday since we talked…

The more Gina contemplated the weekend, however, the more she realized there were deeper questions to be answered. The answers to those questions, might not be as easy to overcome as simply as the physical reconnection had been.

She pushed the thoughts to the back of her mind. *I've got plenty of time to think through that later. Today, I need to get home, check on the kids, and get ready for Monday.*

Monday, Monday…. back to Melvin and volunteer work. Really, how happy am I with my life? It sure seems that Jo's done a lot more satisfying things with hers…

She turned on the music, her Elvis CD still playing.

That's it…. Elvis and the road home…

Gina turned into her drive only seconds before Melvin. She had missed him over the weekend, but only in a lukewarm way. And right at this moment, she didn't want his company. She was preoccupied with her thoughts and trying to reconcile questions that a friendship with Jo was apparently begging to be answered. She didn't want to be bothered with Melvin.

Now, how am I gonna tell him, nicely, to go home?

"Hey, sweetheart. Looks like we timed that perfectly. Hard day at the diner? Jo and I had the best time…I wish you could've gone."

Melvin stopped to plant a kiss on her cheek.

"Well, I can't up and leave on the weekend, especially summer weekends. It's our busiest time. But I'm glad you two enjoyed yourself. I brought leftovers for supper, you hungry?"

"Yes, I am. We didn't eat much since lunch and traveling always makes me hungry. What ya got?"

"It's basically a hodge-podge of stuff I threw together on a couple of take-out plates. It'll be easier to show ya – here, you take the plates and I'll get your stuff."

Gina took the plates from him and headed for the door, her phone's insistent ringing in her purse made her smile.

Probably the grandkids. I'll call 'em back when I get in the house.

As she made her way to the door, she called back to Melvin.

"Get the big bag, I can get the little one in the morning. I don't need them tonight anyway."

As she unlocked the door and sat the plates down, she pulled her phone from her purse. Not the kids, it was her dad.

Mmm… that's unusual for a Sunday afternoon.

She punched the "Dad" button and waited for him to answer. His voicemail was her only greeting.

Melvin was by now inside with the luggage and eyeing the plates, as if to say "well, aren't you gonna open them?"

"Melvin, that was dad that tried to call and now he's not answering.

You wanna ride with me over to check on him? May not be anything, but he just called… he should've answered."

Melvin released a long sigh.

"No, I really don't. I've been up and at work since 5 this morning, and I don't really wanna go anywhere but here or home."

"Well, I need to run check on him. He did have that accident Friday. Something might be wrong. Let me try him one more time."

Once again, the call went to voicemail.

"I gotta go; thanks for the food. Go on home and I'll call you in a little while."

A rather disgruntled but obliging Melvin followed her out the door.

"Alright, Gina. Call me and let me know you made it back home. And if something is wrong, let me know that too."

"I will, talk to you in a bit."

Gina locked the door behind them and in a few seconds was seated behind the wheel again.

The jumbled houghts of the weekend and the unresolved issues with Jo had been replaced with worry for her dad.

What if the accident really did hurt him, maybe internally? Something that I didn't see on Friday? He didn't sound too good this morning when I talked to him…

As she left the driveway, she placed a call to Millie.

"Millie, hey baby. I made it home ok, but Pawpaw's not answering his phone. I'm gonna run over and check on him. Did you have to work this weekend? How are the girls?"

"No, I didn't work this weekend, but David did. The girls and I have been hanging out at home. So far, Henley Jane has competed in her own Olympic games, and Bella Kate managed to save a baby bird." Millie chuckled. "A typical weekend at our house. Did you have a good time with Aunt Jo? Reckon what's wrong with Pawpaw? I stopped by yesterday, but no one was home."

"Oh, I'm not sure honey. It may be nothing, but he tried to call me, and I couldn't get to the phone. When I tried him back, he wasn't answering. I wanna check on him."

"Ok, well, call me if you need me mom. Otherwise, I'll talk to you tomorrow. Love ya."

"Love you too, tell my babies Ginny says hey, and I love them."

"I will. Bye Mom."

By the time she finished her conversation with Millie, she was almost to her dad's. Once Millie said she had stopped by to check and no one was home, Gina became a little more concerned.

Now, they towed his truck to the service center and we got him a rental Friday. Where could he have gone on Saturday unless it was the diner?

When she pulled into the drive, she saw the rental car.

So why didn't he answer the phone?

Gina didn't even bother to knock. Opening the door, she called out to him "Dad? Dad? Where are you?"

He called to her from his bedroom.

"Gina? Is that you? Come here, help me. Thank goodness, I couldn't get to the phone after I called you… I dropped it."

When she reached the bedroom, it was a chaotic sight that greeted her.

Her dad had carried the step ladder into the bedroom, apparently to replace a light bulb over the bed. He was a few feet from the bed, his phone, off to his right, was out of reach, and the step ladder lay tumbled on top of them both.

"Dad! Good heavens! What were you doin'? What were you thinkin'? Is anything broken? Are you ok?" The questions tumbled out much faster than Mr. Floyd could even begin to answer.

"Aw, I've messed up my leg, but other than that, I'm ok. Can you help me get up, let me see if I can stand? I couldn't get myself out from under everything."

Gina moved the ladder, trying to get it off her dad without doin'g any further damage to the leg that was threaded through the steps.

"Ahhh…. jeez, that hurts. Go slow, girl. Slow. I'm pretty sure it's broken. Dammit."

Gina had lots of things she wanted to say, such as "what on earth possessed you to even try to change the light? For Christ's sake, you're almost 80. Somebody else can change the bulb." But she didn't. She held those thoughts for later.

"Here, Daddy, be still. Give me a minute and I'll go really slow gettin' this ladder off you. First though, I'm callin' Melvin. He's gonna have to help me get you to the hospital."

And so went Gina's Sunday night and Monday morning.

Melvin wasted no time in arriving to help and Gina stayed with him in Emergency until they could get him admitted and in a room.

X-rays confirmed that it was broken, right below the knee.

Finally, in the wee hours of Monday morning they gave him enough pain medicine to put him to sleep. The doctor scheduled surgery for Tuesday, and Gina decided to make her way home.

Exhaustion didn't really describe the tiredness that overtook her on the way home.

Lord, give me strength. These next few years are gonna take their toll. How do you fill the roles? Mom, daughter, caregiver, grandmother, friend, advisor. Never mind anything I want to do…

She slipped between the sheets at 4:15.

When she finally woke Monday, it was already 10. She headed for the kitchen and the coffee. She was gonna need the caffeine this morning. As soon as she had gulped enough to find clarity of thought, she called the North Arkansas Ozark Family Services Center.

I hope and pray I don't have any volunteer work today.

The receptionist answered the phone and Gina took enough time to cover the 'Hey how are you' greetings, then asked if there was anything on the schedule for her today.

Fortunately, there was not. Tuesday at 3pm was the first activity Gina had scheduled with a young lady named Marcie.

Thank goodness. Now, to check on Dad.

She spent her Monday morning taking care of the issues that Floyd's fall had created at his house. Monday afternoon, she would need to be back at the hospital.

Somewhere in amongst the errands and resolution of issues, she called Millie and Melvin.

"Millie, Pawpaw broke his leg. That's why I couldn't get him to the phone. I don't have time right now for details, but I won't be home to get the girls off the bus. Can you or David get them?"

"Oh, Mom. Where is he now? The hospital? I'm workin', but David can get them. Let me call him. Call me back this afternoon, do I need to come?"

"No, not yet. They're supposed to operate tomorrow and I may need you then. Just wait, let's see how it goes. Love ya, sweetheart. I'll call you tonight. And, would you please call Jax?"

Then on to Melvin. It was lunchtime. He was busy.

I knew that. Why did I even call right now?

As she pulled into the hospital parking lot, she realized she hadn't stopped to eat. The hospital cafeteria would still be open.

She was already tired again.

By Wednesday, when she called Jo, she was ready for a break. The thought of coffee and a visit with Jo comforted her.

Please don't let her be busy. I really need a chat with her.

Jo sounded as pleased to hear from her as she had been to call. Thursday morning was still good. Krusty Kupp, coffee and conversation, 9am. She took the time to give Jo the news about Mr. Floyd, but only the highlights. The rest could wait til tomorrow.

Finally, Wednesday night, Gina ran a tub of hot water, turned on the stereo and gave herself time to reflect on their friendship. The magnitude of the unresolved differences from the weekend, as well as the many happy moments returned to her immediate thoughts.

As she soaked, she contemplated.

Why am I even trying? I've got a great life, without her holier than thou bullshit opinions.

Max and Maxine are wonderful people – what does she really even know about them? She doesn't even try to understand their side.

What does she understand when it comes to family and sacrifice? She didn't even try to have one – she doesn't know what it's like to see people's faults but love them anyway.

Work-aholic doesn't even begin to describe Jo – she doesn't know anything except the military – life in the real world doesn't revolve around cyberspace...

But.... we were once so close.... we once shared everything... we had the same views... is it worth it to try to be friends again?

Remember, Gina – it's hard to hate up close....

Her mother's words echoed through her mind. How many times had she returned to those words to overcome misunderstandings, preconceived beliefs, or to try to understand many of the people she met through the rehab program?

At the end of the soak, she was no closer to answers than she had been at the beginning.

To heck with it. I'm just gonna see where it goes. Yes, we're different now. But she is still important to me. She was once my best friend. I enjoy talking to her. No need to hurry and rush a judgment. It might work itself out...

The meeting at the Krusty Kupp on Thursday became a regular habit for them. A habit that included a couple of hours a week with coffee and conversation that revolved around Maureen and Floyd, and the week's planned activity. It gave them a chance to find something they both needed: a woman to talk to and confide in. Someone that knew their past, understood most of their present, and hadn't ruled out a shared tomorrow.

As June wound down they were at their usual Thursday morning coffee date, and Gina brought up the possibility of hiking during the July 4th holiday.

"We haven't talked about it since we got back from the first hike, but you wanna go for the 4th and hike Hemmed In Hollow? Millie, David, and the kids will be up there camping, too."

"Oh, Gina. I'm still having nightmares of the first episode. Sometimes my ankle still twinges and reminds me I am not as young as I used to be."

"Oh, c'mon. You don't have any other plans, do you? You're just gonna sit at home and do nothing. I bet Miss Maureen's goin to Stella's for the weekend."

"She is... and I cannot spend an entire weekend with Stella. Not yet, anyway. What's Mr. Floyd doin'? You gonna leave him by himself?"

"No, he and a bunch of his coffee buddies always get together and grill out for the 4ᵗʰ. They reminisce and talk relive old times. I went once, but whew! They're not my cup of tea. Too many old men, with old tall tales that I've already heard a million times… no thanks!"

Jo laughed. The thought of a bunch of old guys together cooking and trying to outdo each other with the biggest lie was comical.

"Alright, I'll go one more time – but there are conditions. No slippery moldy rocks. No ziplining this time. And last, but not least, no confrontation with Max and Maxine."

"Well, the first two I can promise. But, Jo, you know as well as I do, nobody can promise what a seventy year old man is gonna say or not say. I can promise to *try* to keep the conversation pleasant."

"Where is the Hemmed In Hollow trail? I can't remember where that one starts."

"Yes, you do. It's over by the Steel Creek trail. Steel Creek follows the water and Hemmed In Hollow follows the bluff. Remember?"

"No. It's been too long. Are we gonna stay at the cabins with Max and Maxine?"

"No, it's too far, and the Park has a few cabins they maintain that are closer to the trails and the campground where Millie and David stay. I'd rather stay there, if that's ok with you. I can call Millie and get her to make reservations for us. But I better do it today, it's only a couple of weekends away, and they'll fill up fast."

"Alright, go ahead and make reservations. We'll give it another go with the weekend hiking."

As they were wrapping up their morning coffee and chat, Jo's phone rang. "Maggie" stared at her from the screen.

Oh, lord, I forgot to call them last night, again!

"Hey, Maggie. I guess I forgot you guys last night."

"Yes, you did. We waited and waited. No Jo. No call. You're beginning to make us really paranoid about being your friend. Is everything alright?"

"Yes, I'm fine. I had a really busy week. I'm headed home now, let me call you back tonight. I promise I won't forget again."

"Alright, just wanted to check on you. Talk to you tonight."

Jo stood to go.

"Gina, I gotta go. Class starts at 1, and I still need to finish the lesson for today. Do you need me to do anything to get ready for the 4th? You got it?"

"Yeah, I got it. Just pack your bags! I'll be over the same as before, but we'll still need to take your jeep – my turn to buy the gas!"

Before Jo could call herself ready to leave for another hiking excursion there was a conversation she needed to have with Stella. Stella had turned out to be anything but the attentive eldest child. Jo felt it was time for them to have a frank discussion to discuss Maureen and the role each daughter needed to play in their mother's life.

I don't mind doin'g my part, but I need Stella to help. She seems so unconcerned. I've got to make her understand that something is wrong, and we've got to spend more time taking care of Mom.

Now, she needed to decide how to work the call into her day. Lately, she had more scheduled weekly calls than she had ever experienced on a personal level. There were calls to her mom every morning; calls to George and Maggie on Wednesday nights; and calls between she and Paul sporadically throughout the week.

Although Jo had confided in Paul during their first call, the remaining conversations had been nothing but light hearted coffee table conversation. She just wasn't ready or willing to deal with anything more than that right now.

I have enough to ponder between Mom, Gina, and Stella. I don't need to add a relationship with Paul to the mix. At least not yet.

Even though their conversations were light, Jo instinctively felt a bond with Paul. A bond left over from years ago. Apparently, Paul enjoyed the conversations as much as Jo. There was the possibility he felt it too. Perhaps that's why he continued to call her as regularly as she called him.

She pulled herself out of her reverie to concentrate on the decision at hand: when to call Stella. Tonight wasn't good – she needed to talk to George and Maggie.

And that's something else. Seems that lately, every time I call, they're together. What is going on with my friends? What am I missing by not being there with them? I hope their visit around Labor Day will shed light on what I can't see through a phone line.

Tomorrow. I'm going to call her tomorrow.

Thursday night Jo spent several hours in conversation with George and Maggie. The topics ranged from work issues to teaching schedules. Jo noticed, once again, they were together on a week night at George's apartment.

"Ok, guys. The last several times I've talked with either one of you, you're always together. What gives? What's goin' on there in Washington? Anybody wanna enlighten me?"

Jo heard Maggie chuckle.

"No, Jo. Nothing's up. We just always try to get together for your calls; you know how much we *luuuvvvv* to talk to you!"

Jo couldn't tell if George was mocking her or Maggie since Maggie had a tendency to overuse the word "love" and often pronounced it "luv".

"Whatever. You're hiding something. You two are up to something. But, since you don't wanna answer that question, let's talk about when you're coming to visit. Labor Day still a go?"

As soon as Jo had finished her sentence there was an excited Maggie that responded.

"Yes ma'm! We're still coming Labor Day. I've got my hiking boots shined and ready for a road trip. I have got to get outta this place for a weekend. The work and stuffiness here is almost more than I can bear!"

"Yeah, right. Let me tell you something, Jo. Maggie does not work as hard as you did. She's forever trying to take a break and spends more time bending my ear than she does working on hacker activity. She's such a wuss!"

Jo heard them both laugh aloud and found that it was contagious. Soon, the three of them were laughing as though they were sitting around a table in a bar in Washington.

The beep of an incoming call pulled Jo out of the conversation with them long enough to determine that Paul was on the other line.

"Oops, sorry guys. I'm gonna have to go. Got another call. I'll talk to you next week on Wednesday night. Miss you both! Talk to you then!"

And with that, they said their goodbyes and were gone. Jo felt as deflated as a popped balloon after the calls with George and Maggie. She really did miss them. Not the work, just them.

Now, to return Paul's call.

CHAPTER 11

When you're weary…and feelin' small…
When tears are in your eyes…I will dry them all
I'm on your side…Oh, when time gets rough
And friends just can't be found…
When you're down and out…
I'll take your part….
Like a Bridge over troubled water…

Elvis Presley

JO WAS READY BY 5:30. They were leaving on Monday before the 4th. She wasn't sure if she was looking forward to a holiday, or dreading the possibility of another hiking adventure. At any rate, sleep had been hard to find, and by 3, she'd given up altogether.

She called Gina at 5.

"You ready to go?"

"No, I only got up fifteen minutes ago. Are you already ready? This early?"

"Yeah, I couldn't sleep. Get ready and c'mon. I'll drive – you can finish your coffee and pull everything together on the way."

Gina was in the driveway by 5:45.

"You'll have to excuse the look. It's called 'Jo called and made me hurry', stunning, uh?"

She was grinning from ear to ear.

"I love these getaways. And, I'm gonna get to shoot fireworks with my grandbabies this time."

"C'mon. Let's get this show on the road."

Jo cranked the jeep while Gina threw her bags in the back.

"Ok" she said as she slammed the door, "let's go!"

The drive up this time although just as beautiful was a much warmer drive. In fact, it was downright hot.

"No air conditioner, Jo?"

"Sure, but what's the point, the tops down, the windows are down, why bother with the air conditioner?"

"This reminds me of that year we went to Little Rock shopping in mom's red car. There wasn't an air conditioner in it. You remember?"

"Of course I remember – that's the year we got those god-awful psychedelic mini-skirts and those huge platform shoes."

"Yep. Lord, we thought we were so cool."

"We were. We didn't realize how ridiculous cool looked back then."

"My daddy hated that skirt. He never forbid me to wear it, but he sure did want too. Momma would always say, 'now Floyd, you're not a girl growing up today… they only want to fit in with today's crowd."

"Yeah, daddy would get up and leave the room if I came downstairs wearing mine. He never said a word after that first day I brought it home. He had plenty to say that day, but not afterwards. I figure Mom must have intervened as well."

"Can you imagine what we might have done back then, if we'd had the cell phones of today?"

"Yeah, we would have stayed in trouble for talking and texting constantly. I'm kinda glad we didn't have them, Gina. Look at the issues with young people and sexting, never mind all those internet predators that lurk out there."

"And they don't realize that stuff never goes away – thirty years from now, somebody somewhere, will have one of those pictures. By then, they'll be somebody's mom, or wife, and the consequences could be devastating."

"Speaking of stuff that never goes away, I've spent a lot of time thinking through our first trip a few weekends ago. And I've come to several conclusions. Would you like to hear them?"

Gina was a little apprehensive. She was so in hopes this trip wouldn't be as difficult as the first. Not that they hadn't had a great time, they did. But she didn't want to be on the opposite side of Jo's beliefs on this trip. On this trip, she wanted them to be as they once were. All for one, and one for all.

"Yes…" she said somewhat hesitantly, "Yes, I would like to hear them, but only if the conclusions aren't going to be something that causes us to disagree. We need to have a weekend where we don't have any cross words."

"You're not going to be disappointed. At least not when it comes to my conclusions, that is – there's no way to make any promises for the weekend, especially if it's going to include Max."

Gina chuckled. "You shouldn't be so hard on Max. He's an old man, and harmless. It's ok for someone to have a different view and a different perspective. And it's ok for Max to voice those opinions; it doesn't have to change yours. You know Momma used to always say 'Gina, it's hard to hate up close'."

"I had forgotten that. I used to always wonder exactly what she meant by that when I was a kid. Now, it makes such perfect sense. I always wondered 'up close to what'? Amazing what a little hindsight will do for clarity. And now, for my conclusions…"

"Wait a minute. One more question before you share your conclusions. I'll forget if we get started on conclusions, so I need to ask this question now. How was your mom before we left? Did you check on her?"

"Oh, yes. I went by yesterday to check on her and make absolutely certain that Stella was coming down to pick her up and take her to spend the holiday with them. I even called Stella to confirm. Oh, and speaking of Stella, let me tell you! We finally had our heart-to-heart concerning Mom. She's unbelievable! Don't let me forget to tell you, it happened last Friday and was quite a revelation! As for Mom, physically she's doin'g pretty good. Her leg has healed great, it's her mind that has me worried now. And it's not just that she's forgetful – sometimes the whole direction of a conversation changes, as if you were turning off a light switch. She will bring up one subject, and before we can finish – she forgets – she moves on to something entirely different. I guess I need to do a little research because I can't seem to figure her out."

"I've already researched. Have you had her checked for Alzheimer's, Jo?"

"No… I mean, there's no history of it in our family, that I'm aware of… and I don't think… well, hell, I don't know. You think that's what it might be? I'm not familiar enough with the symptoms. I guess I need to check that out and schedule her for a general checkup. She hasn't had one since she broke her leg."

"I printed several articles and pamphlets for you to read. She's reached the age where it's a possibility and you won't be sure unless you have her checked."

"Ok, give me the materials, and when we get back, I'll read over them and take her to the doctor. Now, on to my conclusions."

"I'm not sure what I expected when I saw your Facebook friend request. To be honest, Gina, so much was happening with my move and mom's health that I hadn't given a lot of thought to anybody in Polk Ridge. Never mind having a chance to get together with you again. That doesn't sound like much of a friend, but that's the truth. Then, when you sent the request, I immediately thought of the Gina from 1976. I didn't stop to consider that we had changed – both of us – not only me and not only you."

"Then, when we met at the house, our conversation was focused on when we were kids. Those conversations barely skimmed the surface though. We didn't talk in terms of 'now'; we talked about 'then'. Once we planned that weekend hike and actually spent a weekend together, reality hit me. The realization that we've both changed over the last forty years, was right there in front of me."

"Oh, Jo. Sure we've changed, but…"

"No, wait. Hear me out. I don't know how you were a counselor, your listening skills suck." She grinned at Gina and picked up with the rest of her conversation.

"When we got home that Sunday, I was having second thoughts. I mean real, second thoughts. Your views and mine are not the same. There are differences in principles, tons of differences in lifestyles, and I wasn't sure what I wanted to do. Then, you know what I did? You're not gonna believe this part… I called Paul."

"You did what? Paul Collections? You called him? For what?"

"Well, I wanted to talk to somebody that didn't know either of us now, somebody that remembered what we were then. To be honest, I'm not sure why I thought of Paul. And, I felt like an idiot at first, trying to talk to him and share our weekend information. But the longer I talked, the more comfortable I felt; it was as if I was talking to the same Paul from so many years ago. With one exception: his voice sounds old!"

Jo laughed, almost girlishly.

"You are unbelievable! I think you still have feelings for Paul. I mean, the first chance you had to run to Paul for advice, that's exactly what you did. That sounds as if it's something to me."

"Well, I'm still sorting that out – that has nothing to do with my conclusions, though. His advice to me: stop looking for Gina Ingram, Class of '76, and start looking for the chance to get to know Gina Phillips, 2012."

"So, I guess I sort of owe you an apology. I expected you to still be the person you were then. I never stopped to think that you've lived a lifetime; a life that I wasn't part of, and I need to get to know the Gina sitting beside me. It might one day be like it was then, or, it might one day be an even better friendship than it was then. However it might turn out, I do want to give it a shot. I can try to understand your side if you can try to understand mine. If there are differences, we'll take them one at a time. To have a friend, you must be a friend."

"Oh, Jo. That's one of the kindest things anyone's ever said to me." There were tears in Gina's eyes, as she looked across the jeep at her old friend.

She quickly swiped at her eyes, smiled and replied, "You always were such a deep thinker. You always had to sort things out over weeks instead of days. I came to these same conclusions in a hot tub of water listening to my Elvis album. You called Paul, I called Elvis. And, discussing Paul Collections is not over – I've got a lot of questions, and we've got a lot of miles to cover this weekend. It's also my turn to drive."

Jo pulled over at the next exit, to hand the wheel over to Gina and take a quick restroom break. When they came back to the jeep, both women had a much rosier outlook for the weekend. Conversation turned toward Maureen and Floyd.

"You said you had talked to Stella. How did that conversation go? Does she understand what's happening with your Mom?"

"No, and to be honest Gina, I can't make her understand. When I called her last Friday to share the fact that I needed her help with Mom, she launched into this long list of excuses. Excuses that covered everything from the demands of running a household, raising boys, to how Jack doesn't seem to understand her anymore. I understand that she's busy and has a family, but she also has a mother."

"I did learn a lot when it comes to things such as Alzheimer's during my years as a social worker. Most children can't seem to reconcile themselves to aging parents and the caregiving demands that accompany those changes. They get stuck in the fact that their parents have always been the caregiver. Reversing roles is a difficult milestone for children to cross. Although Stella has a valid point – she is trying to raise a family – she also might not *want* to deal with Miss Maureen. So, she chooses not to believe there's a problem."

"Well, she's gonna have to come to terms with it. This is not something I can do by myself. I mean, I guess I would if I were an only child. How do you cope with it Gina? You don't have anybody else to help you. It's just you to take care of Mr. Floyd. What do you do?"

Gina gave Jo a rather blank stare.

"Jo, I've never gave it much thought. I mean, I've always known I would have to take care of Dad. There was no one else to help, so I've never considered sharing the care. We're in kinda different positions here. I never considered that either."

Both women were silent for a few minutes. The realization of the responsibility of caregiving was weighing on them, along with the fact that they were once again reminded of the differences of their situation.

"Actually, that statement I made is not entirely true. It's not just me. I have Jax and Millie; and at times, they have been a real help with Dad. Whenever Jax and Vicky come home from Little Rock, they usually stay with Dad. Jax spends at least half of his time during his visit taking care of things around the apartment for Dad. Millie never fails to go by on the weekends and check on him. And then there's times such as this weekend when he spends time with his friends and that helps to really *help* me. It gives me a break and breathing room. Does Miss Maureen ever visit with friends or the grandkids?"

"I suppose she did until here lately. The fact that I've been gone for so long doesn't help me to understand what she needs either, Gina. I guess Stella thinks it's my turn. She's been the one that was here so many years and took care of little things for Mom. She's visited with her, spent holidays with her and I'm sure she brought the boys to spend time with their grandmother when they were small."

"Jo, this may be a bigger issue for you than for Stella because it's a new role for you. Stella may not see it as a big deal because she's accustomed to being around for Miss Maureen. But it can also mean that she won't notice if things are getting worse for Miss Maureen. Such as her not remembering things, or simply changing conversation mid-stream."

"At the moment, that's my biggest problem, Gina. I can see how much Mom's mind is deteriorating because I haven't been a part of her daily life until recently. I'm trying to talk to Stella, and she isn't hearing me."

"Well, as I said, I printed off a few medical articles for you. I guess you need to go and visit with Stella. Take the information and just tell her, 'Stella, we've got to do something – something is wrong with Mom'. Maybe that will get through to her."

"You're right. If a telephone call isn't working, perhaps an actual visit will. And, hopefully, the time she spends with Mom this weekend will help open her eyes."

"Now, back to your earlier revelation. What on earth possessed you to call Paul Collections for advice? And even more important, how did that conversation go?" Gina didn't even attempt to hide the wicked grin that covered her face. "I wanna hear the whole story!"

"Well, there's not that much to tell. Not yet, anyway. The Sunday night we got home from our weekend up here hiking, Paul must have called. I didn't find the voicemail until Monday morning. It was too coincidental. I thought it was a sign. So on Monday afternoon, especially after a couple of glasses of wine, I was sure it was a sign. Then I felt like an idiot and almost wished I hadn't called."

"So what did he say? In the voicemail, I mean."

"He said he was calling to see how things were going with the cabin and to check on me. Nothing deep and personal, Gina. No juicy voicemail pledging his undying love, if that's what you're looking for me to say. It was simply a very nice, hey-I'm-here-if-you-need-me voicemail."

"So why did you decide to seek advice from Paul? Tell me the reasoning behind this again."

"Because I was struggling with what to do. I mean, that weekend was traumatic for me. When you consider our differences, the argument with Max, and then I nearly kill myself on the side of a mountain – hello! I was having a hard time sorting it out. And, I don't have a ton of friends that I can go to for advice. George and Maggie are busy with Washington, and can't give me impartial advice. For God's sake, Max is George's dad. Paul was the logical choice."

"I don't think logic had a damn thing to do with it."

Again, that wicked grin appeared.

"Well, you can thank your lucky stars it was Paul I decided to call. He reminded me to consider the good things in our friendship. He also reminded me that we shouldn't be too quick to judge a friend off of two days spent in the Ozark Mountains. 'Give it time' he said."

"Yeah, and Paul knows a thing or two when it comes to giving things time, doesn't he? What was it he said forty years ago? 'I can wait, Jo', wasn't that what he said? I guess if he can wait forty years, you can wait a few months to see where this is going, right?" She grinned again.

"Yes, you hateful chit, I can wait a few months." Jo returned the same wicked grin to Gina.

"As for my conversations with Paul, that's all I'm gonna share right now. Mostly because that's all there is to share. We're not revisiting a relationship. We talk wine business, the military, and our parents. That's it."

"Yeah, that's it. That's all. Yeah right."

The conversation reached a lull, they were occupied with their thoughts and the last few miles and minutes of their trip passed by quickly, almost too quickly. The next thing they knew they were pulling into the parking lot at Max and Maxine's store.

"I don't guess I'll ever get used to being surrounded by trees and mountains one minute, and staring at a store, cabins, and crowds the next."

"Yeah, you will. It took me several trips, too. Then, suddenly one time I came and, it was as natural as the mountains to see this place."

"Where did you say we were gonna stay this time? Cabins over by Hemmed In Hollow? Are they part of the park?"

"They are. Now, they're not quite as nice as these, but I stayed there a couple of years ago, and it wasn't that bad. The only drawback: no air conditioning."

"No air conditioning? In July? We'll die."

"No, we won't. We'll be hiking most of the day, and at night, it's not that bad. It cools off a lot from the daytime heat, and it's a shaded area. Not much sun shines on those cabins. You'll see, but we do need a few groceries. Let's run in and eat a bite, visit with Max and Maxine, and grab a few things for the cabin."

Jo groaned and slowly extricated herself from the seatbelt and front seat of the jeep.

"Oh, joy, joy."

"Now Jo, remember, old man – harmless."

"Yeah, yeah."

The two women made their way up the steps and into the store. Lucy was on the register. She looked somewhat surprised and tremendously relieved to see Gina.

"Oh, thank goodness you're here. Please go talk to Max. He and Maxine had a huge fight – a few of the customers even left - I was dying of embarrassment. He won't talk to me, but he'll listen to you Gina. Please go talk to him. Maxine's upstairs and refuses to come down til he apologizes."

"My God – these two are too old to be fightin' – they're not teenagers. Where is he? In the kitchen?"

"Yep." Lucy made a grand gesture towards the kitchen.

"Good luck, and may the force be with you!" She grinned. Already relieved that reinforcements had arrived.

Gina looked at Jo.

"Oh, don't worry, I'll be right here waiting on you." Jo reassured her and cleared up any thought that Gina had of asking her to tag along.

Gina slowly made her way to the kitchen.

This is ridiculous. They are way too old to be fighting at all, much less in front of customers.

She peeped through the kitchen doors.

"Max? Are you back here? Lucy said…"

"Yes! I'm in here. And I'm gonna stay in here, til that woman comes to her senses."

"What happened, Max?" Gina asked rather flatly.

"You can't imagine what she's done! Unbelievable! I don't even know what she's thinkin'. She's gone absolutely crazy!"

"Well, you gonna fill me in? I don't have a clue why you're fightin', but you've got to make up, so what's wrong? Why is Maxine crazy?"

"I'm not so sure we've got to 'make up'; she's told that guy I've been talking to about the cabins, that he can just have them. Won't cost him a thing. Come and take them and start taking care of them. She's crazy if she thinks I'm gonna give them away."

"Why on earth would Maxine tell him that? She knows you two have been negotiating, in fact, I thought it was Maxine that was reluctant to give up the cabins? What's happened?"

At that, Max looked a little sheepish.

"Max…. what's happened?"

"Nothing… nothing really. I had a little spell last Sunday, and now she's gone crazy thinkin' I'm gonna die."

"What kind of spell?"

"Aww, it was nothing. I kinda passed out and couldn't breathe, and then I made the mistake of clutching my chest. It was hurtin' a little, but it was because I got scared, and she just went nuts; she's been talkin' and actin' crazy ever since. And then, this morning she called him and didn't even tell me she was callin'. Well, I lost it. She's my wife, she's not supposed to do shit like that – even if she thinks I'm dying, she needs to talk to me. Not give away our stuff!"

Gina suppressed a genuine laugh. These two were unbelievably hilarious, even in their anger she found them comical.

"Alright, Max. I see what you're sayin', but you've got to understand how Maxine might be worried. I bet she tried to get you to go to the doctor, too, didn't she?"

"Yes, but I don't need to go the doctor. I'm fine now."

"Sure you're ok. You got a medical degree? She probably wouldn't have even thought about callin' that guy, if you would have gone to the doctor. Did you ever consider that?"

Max dropped his head and looked away. "No."

"Have you told the boys what happened?"

"No, and I'm not goin' to either. And she better not. I feel fine today, there may not be anything wrong – I mighta just got too hot BBQ'ing."

"Well, I know one great way to find out – SEE A DOCTOR!"

Max was silent for a few minutes and seemed to be looking at something far, far away.

"You really think I should go see a doctor, Gina? It's probably nothing. That's a wasted trip and money if nothin's wrong."

"No, it's not – it will bring Maxine peace of mind. Max, if she didn't love you, it probably wouldn't have scared her so much; and if she didn't love you, it wouldn't have made her so mad when you refused to go to the doctor. And, she probably wouldn't have called that guy, if she hadn't been so mad. You see how this went wrong, Max?"

"I see you've figured out how to make it my fault, Gina Phillips. You women are the same – you're not happy til it's a man's fault!" As he finished his sentence, there was a smile on his face and a twinkle in his eye.

Gina returned the grin.

"You wanna go make up with Maxine and apologize?"

"No, I don't want to, but I will. You woulda been a great daughter to have Gina. You could sweet talk anybody, but it works especially well on an old man like me."

He stopped to give her a bear hug as he headed for the stairs.

Gina found Jo and Lucy in conversation at the register as she returned from the kitchen.

"Well," Lucy said, "I didn't hear an explosion. How'd it go? Those two been at each other since Sunday when Max fell out. I thought Maxine was gonna hyperventilate on the spot. I've never seen her so flustered and upset."

Jo didn't comment at that moment. That would come later.

"Oh, they're old, stubborn, and love each other way too much.

Max went upstairs, and Maxine will probably be making him a doctor's appointment shortly."

"Now, on to more pressing issues – we need lunch and groceries to take to the cabins this weekend. We're hikin' Hemmed In Hollow."

Jo and Gina spent the next hour chatting with Lucy, eating lunch and gathering groceries. It was well into the afternoon as they left the store and drove over to the cabin Gina had asked Millie to reserve.

Gina picked up her phone to call Millie and get the cabin number as Jo cranked the jeep and they left the parking lot.

The phone rang only once before Millie's cheery "Hello".

"Millie, mom here. What cabin did you reserve for us?"

"Uh-oh. I knew there was something else I was supposed to do. Let me call you right back." She never gave Gina a chance to answer as she heard the click on the other end.

"Uh… Jo, we might have a small issue. I am guessing Millie forgot to make reservations for a cabin. Oh dear, and this is the 4th of July week. Lord, I hope they've got an empty cabin. I didn't bring a tent and I sure don't want to share with Millie and David."

"No, we're not gonna share with Millie and David, and I'm not camping in a tent, anyway. No, no, not me. Cabin or we go home or come back here. It's that simple."

C'mon, Jo, you don't wanna rough it? Nothing like a tent, mountain air, and the great outdoors." She laughed. She already had the answer to that question. One look at Jo's face and it was clear: it would either be a cabin or they would be headed back to Polk Ridge.

They had reached the entrance to the campgrounds and Hemmed In Hollow Trailhead. As they left the highway, there was a big stone structure that held the sign "Hemmed In Hollow Trail and Campgrounds". The road that led to the trailhead had been paved and lined with crepe myrtles the first fifty or sixty feet. The natural hardwood of the forest took over as soon as the crepe myrtles ended. Another hundred yards, and the forest gave way to a green field. To the right there was a small log structure and a sign that said "Registration Post". To the left was thirty camp sites, complete with grills and picnic tables for each occupant.

As they pulled the jeep onto the dirt lot at the end of the pavement, Gina's phone rang.

"Ok, I got you a cabin – it's not one of the newer ones – but it's a cabin, just the same. Where are you guys now?"

"Pulling in to the Trailhead, I can see the registration post now. Which cabin did you get, Millie?" Gina gave Jo a sideways glance. She also crossed her fingers and hoped it wasn't the cabin they called "Hemmed Up Hell".

"Number 26, it's at the base of the bluff – right before you start up the Hemmed In Hollow bluff trail."

"Oh no, not that old cabin! Millie, how could you forget? It's as old as I am! I don't think it's even got running water!"

"Yes, it does. They added runnin' water a couple of years ago. It's not that bad – they've upgraded it since we last stayed there. Remember what we called it then?"

"Yes, I remember – I was hopin' it wouldn't be that one!"

All during their exchange, Jo glared at Gina.

This wasn't going as either woman had hoped.

Jo began to shake her head.

"Alright Millie, where's the key? Is it at the registration post?"

"Yes, it will be hanging with the rest of the keys or at least on a hook where the other keys should be. Call me back if it's not there and I'll see what I can do to unlock it and let you in."

"Alright, I gotta run. Talk to you in a bit."

Gina ended the call, and Jo ended her silence.

"Where are we stayin? It doesn't have runnin' water? Seriously, no runnin' water?"

"Yes, it does now. Although it didn't at one time. Cabin #26, at the base of the Hemmed In Hollow bluff. It's a very old cabin, but Millie says they've repaired and upgraded and it's in much better shape than the last time I stayed there."

"Well, what did you remember, you know when you stayed there last? When you were on the phone with Millie."

Gina hesitated. She didn't wanna tell Jo what they called it. That would only set her off again.

"We nicknamed the cabin. We called it 'Hemmed Up Hell'."

Jo's face was crimson. Gina knew it was from holding back the flow of disparaging words.

"And pray tell, *why* did you call it that, Gina?"

Gina could only laugh. It was a laugh that comes from deep within, and bursts forth uncontrollably, rolling on for what seemed forever, the kind you simply can't stem or stop.

She couldn't wait to tell Jo "why".

CHAPTER 12

Day after day I'm more confused
Then I look for the light through the pourin' rain...
Dobie Gray

AS GINA GASPED FOR breath in between roarous laughter, Jo steered the jeep toward the registration post to register and check for the key. She didn't see the extreme humor of the situation.

"When you finally manage to get a grip on yourself, would you please tell me where to look for a key? And please, please share what you find so humorous with a nickname that includes the word 'hell'."

Gina had no trouble detecting the sarcasm in Jo's comment.

"Alright, Jo. I'm trying to stop. Mm… guess you had to be there. Let me tell you about the nickname after we find the key and start to the cabin. You know we're gonna have to walk part of the way, right?"

"Hell no, I didn't know we were gonna have to walk to the cabin; how would I? How many years has it been since I was in the Ozarks? Did I ever hike this area? How could I possibly know that?"

Jo was growing more irritated with every passing minute and sentence.

"Ok, ok. Calm down, please. It's not that far, and we don't have too much to carry. Chill out. Let me go see if the keys are hanging on the hook."

Gina hopped from the jeep as if she were running from the devil himself.

Whew! She needs to calm down. Then I can tell her about the cabin, and maybe she will find it as funny as we did. NOT.

She reached the registration post and began to look for the key. There it was, hanging alone. The other cabin keys were gone.

Gee thanks, Millie. We got it because nobody else wanted it. What is that girl thinkin' of these days? She's got to where she doesn't remember anything I say.

Gina returned to the jeep, key in hand.

"I got it – it was hangin' right where she said it would be. And, I filled out the registration slip – we're good to go."

"Go where? I don't see a road, a cabin, or a sign. Where are we supposed to go from here?"

"If you'll pull on past this registration post, way over there to the right is a parking area. The trail that leads to most of the cabins, including #26, begins in that parking area. Our cabin is at the very beginning of the ascent up the bluff; the river is only a few hundred feet from where we'll be stayin'. It really is beautiful there. There are, however, two drawbacks: everybody that hikes the trail will come by the cabin, and it's as old as you and I."

Jo let out a deep sigh. One that was mixed with exasperation as well as desperation.

She was trying to follow Paul's advice. She also recognized that this weekend had the potential to turn into a complete disaster once again.

"Alright, let's get the stuff and get started. Our packs aren't goin' to carry themselves to the cabin, and I could use a chair and a cigarette. On the upside, a beautiful mountain sunset might help my disposition."

"See? Jo, that right there is one of the reasons we were such good friends back in the day. You always could find the silver lining to any cloudy day. Better than I could. I need a friend that see's the glass as half-full, not half-empty."

Gina was reaching for her packs and the groceries as Jo prepared to lock the jeep; she had already set her gear to the side and reached in her bag for her pack of cigarettes.

"I'll have a smoke before we start, that way I'll huff and puff while we're toting our gear like pack mules into the wilderness to stay in a cabin that probably resembles a mountain man's shack. I am beginning to *clearly* see the humor in this. Now, if we could only run into a bear along the way, our day would be complete."

"Ha-ha – funny girl. We are going to have a good time – even if it kills us." Gina threw her pack over her shoulder, smiled at Jo, and started for the trail.

"You can catchup when you finish smoking – there's only one way in and one way out. When you do catchup, I'll tell you what was so funny the last time I stayed here."

Jo sucked hard a couple of times on the cigarette, stomped it out, and then hurried to catch Gina. At the very least, she deserved to hear a funny story.

"Wait, wait! I'm comin'. Now tell me what was so damn funny earlier."

Gina began to relay the story of Hemmed Up Hell for Jo.

"It started 5 years ago. Millie had been working as a Park Ranger for several years, and David had been in Administration at the Park Office in Jasper. This particular summer, they were short on Park Rangers, and David volunteered to take summer duty. They never dreamed they would both be expected to work the 4th of July holiday, but as it turned out they were scheduled to work. They had nobody to watch the girls. Nobody, that is, unless I would come up here and camp with them. I could watch the girls during the day, and we could spend our nights at a cabin. As Millie put it 'we'd have quality family time'. Well, we did. And that's where things got out of control."

"The first day we were here, we discovered that Cabin #26 had no running water. We also discovered that it had no air conditioning. I had two little girls that were 3 years old. You know how hard it is to tend to children in the middle of the summer when you don't have water or cold air?"

"We tried to get another cabin, no luck. They were full because of the holiday. So, then I decided I'd take them swimming to keep from bein' so hot during the day – big mistake. I'm not 25 anymore and trying to keep up with them in a river is not possible. They wouldn't stay together, they didn't want to play on the rocks or the sand. It was a small disaster. Finally, after lunch that first day I talked them into looking for flowers and animal tracks around the cabin. I thought it was a great idea. Get them interested in nature, blah, blah blah."

"I sense a 'but' in here somewhere."

"Oh, yes. A huge 'but'. I had no idea that Bella Kate would actually find and catch a wild animal. And not just any wild animal: a skunk. She thought it was a cat."

"Oh dear God! What did you do? Did she really catch it?"

"Oh yeah, she caught it, and brought it right on back to the cabin to show me. How that skunk didn't spray her, I'll never know – but by the time she got to me, it was primed and ready."

"Oh, Gina. Oh my goodness. What did you do?"

"Well, the minute she rounded the corner at the cabin, Henley wanted to hold it too; that must have been the final straw for the poor little skunk. Just as she reached to try to take him from Bella Kate and I stepped closer to tell her to let it go, NOW, the skunk doused us all!"

"It was horrible! Our eyes were watering, I couldn't breathe for the stench, Bella Kate threw it down, both girls were crying from their burning eyes and nose. It was a sight I'm sure. If we hadn't smelled so bad, it would have been funny. I grabbed them up and headed for the water; I thought we could wash the scent off in the river. Nope. Didn't work."

"By the time Millie and David got there, everything, including the cabin, smelled of skunk. We spent that holiday in misery, I mean misery. After the initial shock of the spraying, the girls didn't seem to notice or mind the smell very much, but the rest of us suffered!"

"It was on the second day that Millie called it 'Hotel Hell', and finally we decided on 'Hemmed Up Hell'. When it was finally over and I got back home, I threw the clothes away – I'd had more than enough of the "skunk" perfume."

"The only upside was the fact that we weren't visited by other hikers; they would get within smellin distance and quickly disappear up the trail. Bella Kate looked at me that third day and said 'Ginny, why don't they stop and come see us?' I don't guess a three-year old is bothered so much by the stench of a skunk!"

"Oh good Lord, Gina. And ya'll stayed, the whole time?"

"Well, yeah we stayed. Millie and David had to work; there weren't any other cabins, and we had no choice. But every year after that, we made it a tradition to spend the 4th up here, only we usually camp in a tent. That way, we can move should Bella Kate rescue another skunk. You can never be sure what that child will drag up from the woods – birds, squirrels, rabbits, and apparently, skunks. Although I will say, she hasn't mistaken them for a cat again!"

They had reached their destination by the time Gina finished her story and Jo was more than a little winded.

"Set your stuff down out here and let's inspect this place before we settle in for the weekend. It is summertime; there might be a wild creature already inhabiting our sleeping space."

Jo's face clearly displayed her displeasure at having to inspect where she was gonna sleep.

"If there's nothing in there now – what's to keep it from coming later?"

"Jo, I don't think we'll be invaded once we're setup, but this cabin has been empty for months – and we're not stayin' in a resort. No one's been in or out to check it – let's just be safe and have a look before we take in all our stuff."

Jo reached for her pack, unzipped the front, and retrieved her .38.

Gina looked askance. "You brought a gun?" You're not supposed to have firearms in a National Park."

"Well, isn't that the pot callin' the kettle black. So, it's okay for you to break the law, but not me?"

"Jo, that's different."

"No it's not. But at least I'm tryin' to protect us, not fly over the tops of the trees."

Gina grinned at her words and winked. "I figure you don't need as much protection if you're flyin' over tree tops!"

"It's not that you don't need it, you just don't notice that you need it from my perspective."

Gina unlocked the cabin door, and they made their way inside, Jo holding steadily to the .38. She might be spending her holiday with nature, but she wasn't going to let it turn life threatening. She briefly contemplated the situation.

It seems life with Gina is more dangerous than all those years I spent in the military. That is so ironic.

Gina went in first, with Jo following. The cabin was empty, except for a couple of bunk beds, a table and an old stove. The room was dim and smelled musty, reminding them of an old basement. Over to their left, there was a sink and a toilet stall. The windows still had wooden shutters that when closed, made the room dark and mysterious. They both looked from side to side and top to bottom. Gina turned to Jo. "Oh, would you put that thing away – see, there's nothing in here."

At that very moment, Jo watched as something slithered down the back wall of the cabin.

"Move, Gina. There's something on the back wall. Sweet Jesus, it's a snake."

"You're imagining that, I didn't see…" and she stopped in mid-sentence. Sure enough, right there against the back wall, right beside the stove, a coiled heap hissed in their direction.

"I told you I saw something."

"I can't see well enough to see what kind it is, can you?"

"Who cares? A snake is a snake. I'm not gonna take the time to ask 'Hey buddy – are you a bad snake or a good snake? You gonna bite us, or just stay for tea?' Move, I'm gonna shoot it."

"No, don't shoot, Jo. Let's see if we can get it to leave."

Jo looked at Gina as though she had grown another head.

"Are you crazy? It's a snake! Move!"

Gina didn't need to hear it again – she moved towards the door as Jo discharged the gun. No more snake.

Once the ringing in their ears subsided, they had removed the snake, and inspected for other family members, they went outside to get their packs and the groceries.

"Alright, Annie Oakley, which bunk do you want? Top or bottom?"

Gina's sense of humor and light mood had returned.

Jo wasn't quite the happy camper, just yet.

"Bottom – you sleep up there with the snakes since you are so fond of them. I'm sleepin' down here, so I can escape if necessary."

"Now, now. I don't think we'll have any more unwanted visitors. He probably only wanted to spend his holiday in peace. The cabin's usually empty, not filled with old women and guns."

"Ha ha – funny. But aren't you glad we had it?"

"Yeah, I guess so. But put it away now and don't tell Millie and David you've got a gun. For heaven's sake, I don't want you to get arrested on this holiday trip and we sure don't need an accidental shooting!"

"Speaking of accidents – how's Mr. Floyd? You haven't mentioned him today."

"Oh, he's fine. His leg is healing up right on schedule, and he's lookin' forward to his holiday visitors."

"Oh, yeah. You said he gets together with his friends on the 4th."

"Yes, and til then, a couple of them are coming by to check on him for me. And then on the 4th they're all meeting there to grill. I don't think there will be a shortage of company for him or tall tales. Old men can come up with mighty big lies! And Dad fits right in. He'll be fine, but I do wanna call and check-in every day – just to be sure."

Both women had unpacked and situated their belongings during the conversation and suddenly looked around to find they had time to do--what?

"It's almost 6, too late to hike, but too early to call it a day. What should we do?" Gina turned to ask Jo, who'd taken a seat on the front porch of the cabin.

"I don't know what you're gonna do, but I brought a bottle of wine and my smokes. I'm gonna sit here on the front porch, enjoy the view and relax."

"Well, I guess we could sit and talk. Let me phone Millie and tell her we got to the cabin. I don't know what they're doin' this afternoon, but it's much too late for a visit."

As Gina called to check in with Millie, Jo retrieved her phone from the cabin. She hadn't taken the time to check for messages or missed calls.

No missed calls, but there were two text messages – one from George, and one from Paul.

George's text simply said "I'm apologizing before my parents do something else and hope you have a good time with Gina."

Paul's was a bit longer, and Jo looked forward to responding. It's possible he wasn't as disinterested in her life as she had first thought…

They sat on the cabin's porch and enjoyed a beautiful mountain sunset. Finally, the day began to calm down and the conversation was focused on shared memories, old and new.

"Gina, my life has been so structured, so anticipated, and without family issues that pull you in different directions. It's a big adjustment to get used to all your ups and downs. You seem to roll with the punches, very seldom out of sorts. That both irritates and amazes me."

"You just get used to constantly changing circumstances, Jo. Life with family, kids, and the losses I've experienced, conditions you to adjust; it's a different spin on 'adapt and overcome', but the result is the same. Not that much different than what you were taught in the military… not when you look at the concept, not the circumstances."

"I guess you're right. I guess I've become too set in my own routine, too controlling to greet changes with a smile."

"The upside is that it's never too late," and she flashed Jo that famous grin. "You've adapted pretty well today."

Jo thought back over the unexpected events of their day.

"I guess you've got a point. I didn't even have a meltdown over the snake."

"No, you didn't. And actually, that was cool. You did learn something besides computers in the military. You're pretty good with a gun, Annie."

"Yes, I can defend myself. Too bad we can't say the same for you."

"Ha, ha. I've managed so far. I'm gonna call Dad while we're settin' out here and I have service."

"Yeah, and I need to call and make sure Stella managed to pick Mom up and get home with her."

Jo didn't mention the text from Paul. No need to give Gina further reason to speculate.

The next hour or so was spent in phone calls and light conversation. It was only the creep of late afternoon shadows that pulled Gina out of her reverie to contemplate food. That and the gnawing of her stomach.

"Alright, time for food and a good night's sleep. Let's go decide what to have and get ready for tomorrow – Hemmed In Hollow won't be easy."

Jo's alarm was the first thing she was aware of as the night had passed them by, both women exhausted from the previous days' activities.

5:30 – time to rise and shine.

Dear Lord, please let this day be calm. Please don't let me strangle Gina over something simple such as hiking Hemmed In Hollow. Amen.

Jo threw back the covers and called Gina. Time for breakfast and a beautiful day in the Ozarks.

Gina was slow to respond, 5:30 was so early. She much preferred to rise around 7, drink a couple of cups of coffee, and slowly welcome the new day. Apparently, with Jo, that was not an option.

She is a control freak. She just can't let go and let the day simply unfold, slowly and haphazardly. Always got to have a plan.

"Gina, wake up, let's get breakfast, and then get started! Daylight's wasting!"

"Uhhh… I'm waking up. Start the coffee… this could take a little while. This bunk bed is definitely not made for fifty year old bones!"

They spent the next hour waking, dressing and eating breakfast. Gina was still pulling her mind from the fog of sleep when Jo began to assemble their backpack.

"Did you bring a map of the trail, Gina? I meant to print one off before we left, but I forgot."

"No, we don't need a map, I know this trail just as good as The Lost Valley Trail. What do you want to know? I *can* say there's no slippery rocks!" She laughed, remembering Jo's roll down the side of the mountain.

"No, I just wanted to know how long it is, if it's classified as 'moderate' or 'easy'. All that necessary hiking information for someone who doesn't do this every year."

"It's neither. This one is classed as 'strenuous'. But don't worry, you'll be fine – we can stop and rest all along the way; there's such beautiful views as you climb the mountain, and once you get to the top – it's just absolutely gorgeous."

"Strenuous? I barely made the moderate hike through Lost Valley. I don't think I'm ready for 'strenuous'. Why didn't you say that when we planned this?"

"Because, it doesn't matter. We've got 3 days to hike it, we don't have to hike the whole trail, and we can stop to rest as much as we want. You'll be fine. Just finish the backpack and let's get started. Don't worry. We won't have any trouble with Hemmed In Hollow."

Jo stared at Gina.

Famous last words?

CHAPTER 13

Will you meet me in the middle?
Just enough to show you care?

America

AS THEY MADE THEIR way up the winding trail of Hemmed In Hollow, conversation was sparse. The effort it took to merely breathe and walk consumed most of Jo's energy. Conversation was low on the list of priorities.

"I thought you said this wouldn't be too bad?"

"It's not. Are you tired? We can stop up the way here. There's a great view and a spot for resting."

Jo was plainly struggling to keep up with Gina. And losing her composure in the process.

"I told you smoking was bad for you. See how much trouble you're having coming up this little hill?"

"Hill hell. This is a mountain, Gina. And it's not the cigarettes; it's not being accustomed to hiking in this environment."

"Yeah, whatever. Excuses, excuses. Ok, let's stop here."

Gina and Jo threw their packs to the ground and settled on a pair of rocks that were just to the side of the trail.

"Water! I need water!"

"Looks like you need a paramedic, really. You sure you're ok?"

"Yes, I'm fine. Slightly winded, but fine. Let's sit here a minute. I'll catch my breath, then we can go a bit further. Speaking of further, how far is it really to the top?"

"It's 3.6 miles to the top of the bluff, then of course 3.6 miles back down. But we're not in a hurry – we've got all day to go up and come down. And coming down is much, much easier than going up."

She smiled at Jo.

Bless her heart. She really is having a tough time. I just didn't realize it would be this hard on her.

"Don't smile that 'I'm-so-sorry-for-Jo-smile'. I'll be fine. If you can hike it, so can I."

"Ok, ok. Yes, you certainly can. I just don't want to be out in the middle of nowhere and you have a heart attack."

"Really, Gina? A heart attack? I'm in better shape than that. It's this 'strenuous' hike that's the problem. I should've checked this out ahead of time."

"You have no spontaneity, Jo. None. Everything must be planned, planned, planned."

This time when she flashed a smile it was the old one. The one Jo remembered.

"Ok, I'm rested enough. I wanna take a pic of this view. My lord, the view of the valley from up here is truly breathtaking!"

From their vantage point on the side of the bluff, they could see for miles across the valley beneath them. It was still early enough that the blue haze of morning hadn't lifted and the greens of the valley seemed to blur into the blue of the sky. A sky that was tinged with pink, purple and white fluffy clouds. The sun peaked at them from behind those same cotton candy fluffs. From here they could also see the Buffalo River as it cut its path through the valley.

"Yeah, it really is beautiful. I remember coming up here not long after Robert died. I was having so much trouble finding peace and beauty in anything. Then I looked out from this exact spot. It suddenly dawned on me how much I had to be thankful for. I had been wallowing in self-pity. Wallowing and feeling sorry for myself. It was sunrise that morning that really woke me up. God gives us the most beautiful and perfect gifts, and we never have to lift a finger. Sunrise on this mountain is one of them. It was a turning point for me. I suddenly felt peace with my life. I still had two wonderful children, a place to live, and hope for a better tomorrow. The pity party was over."

Jo sat in silence contemplating her friend's revelation. She really just couldn't imagine how Gina must have felt. A small part of her aggravation with the hike melted away.

They sat together for another few minutes simply enjoying the view and each other's company.

"Ok, time to go!" it was Gina that broke the silence.

"We gotta get to the top, so we can enjoy the stroll back down! Hopefully, we'll meet Millie along the way. She's usually up and down this trail when she works over here."

With that, they lifted the packs to their backs and made their way further up the trail.

Some two or three hours later, they did cross paths with Millie. It had taken them that long to travel two-thirds of the trail; there had been more than one occasion that both women had to stop, rest and catch their breath.

As they rounded a curve in the trail that opened to a much wider rest stop, Millie came into sight from the opposite end of the trail.

"Hey, Mom! I was hoping I'd run into you two today!"

"Hi, sweetheart. Yes, I told Jo we might get to see you today. Where are the girls? With David?"

"Yes. I took the morning shift, and David's got the afternoon. It was the only way we could accommodate a weekend of camping with the girls. They look forward to this weekend so much, we didn't couldn't disappoint them."

Jo hadn't spoken yet. She was too busy eyeing Millie. She could've passed for Gina's twin. A young Gina's twin. She looked so much like her mother it was a shock to Jo.

I wonder if I had a daughter would she look so much like me.

"Hi, Millie. I haven't seen you since you were a little bitty thing. You are a carbon copy of your mom. Except, well, you seem organized and so cute in that ranger uniform."

She reached to give Millie a hug.

"Aunt Jo, you haven't changed a bit from the photos I've been looking at all these years. You look great! Is mom being difficult? You know how she is – never too much planning on her part!" Millie smiled and then chuckled; that same laugh Gina had.

"Yes, I know your Mom's method of operation quite well. No, we're having a great time. We've only encountered one snake, no skunks, and she hasn't killed me on this bluff, not yet, anyway." Jo returned Millie's infectious smile.

I like her. But of course I would, I like her mom. I can tell though, she's not quite as free-wheeling as Gina.

"How's the morning been? Nothing to report from the ranger's view? No lost hikers, no accidents, no heart attacks?" Gina looked pointedly at Jo.

"No, mom. All's clear so far. I've been checking the trail for distressed hikers or even more distressed animals, and I've found nothing. A wonderful day in the Park! Would you guys like to come over and grill this afternoon? David won't be there, but the girls would love to see their Ginny and meet their great-aunt Jo."

"We'll see. I'll give you a call when we start back down the bluff. It all depends on how long it takes us to get up the trail, coming down will be a breeze. As to whether we come for supper tonight or not,

I can promise you we'll be there for the fireworks tomorrow night. I wouldn't miss that for the world. I love watching Bella Kate and Henley Jane when those fireworks explode. They should absolutely love this holiday!"

"Ok, well, you two be careful. I don't want to have to help my mom or aunt off the bluff because of an accident! I gotta run. Talk to you this afternoon."

Millie turned to go, and Jo turned to take a seat on the bench that had been placed by the side of the trail.

"Gina, she's just like you. Except, she seems a little more organized."

"Actually, Jo, she's a lot more like you than me. She's come out of her shell somewhat now that she's older. But when she was young – she'd rather spend her time in the woods than with people. She's also extremely organized and a complete planner! Nothing is left to chance with that one. Sound familiar?"

"Yeah, that does sound like a great daughter – OF MINE! Not yours. You suppose some of my genes rubbed off on you all those years ago?" Jo laughed. How ironic that she didn't have a daughter, yet Gina's behaved as though she might have been hers.

"Ok, time to go again. Take heart Jo, we're almost there. Only one mile left to go, and it's barely 11 o'clock. We're making great time!"

"Oh, yeah. Great time. I'll be so sore tomorrow I won't be able to move. But, what a great time!"

Gina ignored the sarcasm and started back up the trail.

"C'mon soldier; let's soldier on up this bluff!"

Just as the sun reached its zenith, Jo and Gina reached the top of the bluff. The temperature at the top of Hemmed In Hollow bluff was hovering around 90 degrees. Both women were soaked with sweat when they reached the crest.

"Thank God! It's the top of the bluff. Thank you, thank you – we made it to the top!"

Jo was as exhausted as she had been since… since she couldn't remember when. Her body would definitely make her pay for this tomorrow.

"Yeah! We did it! And we did it in only half a day! That's great!" Gina was elated. Jo wasn't.

"I've got to have food and water and rest. I really can't enjoy any sense of accomplishment right at this moment, Gina. Basic survival needs are overtaking my emotions. What did we bring to eat?"

Gina's color drained from her face.

"I only packed water and a few snacks. I thought you were packing the food."

Now it was Jo's face that changed color. The crimson flush of controlled anger consumed her.

She spoke slowly. "You mean we're on top of this bluff, completely isolated – and all we have are snacks?"

Gina silently and slowly nodded affirmation.

"I packed water and snacks; I told you to pack the foodstuffs."

"No, I thought you said you were packing food, for me to get the water and snacks." Jo still spoke in a very controlled, slow monotone.

"Well, then, if we both packed snacks, we'll be ok."

Gina made a feeble attempt to calm what she could see was an approaching storm.

"Gina, I'm going over to the other side of this trail. I'm going to smoke a cigarette and try to think of nicer things to say. While I'm gone, would you mind removing our snacks from the backpacks? I'd like to determine exactly *what* we have to feast on and we'll try to 'adapt and overcome'."

With that, Jo turned on her heel and hastily walked away. Gina was left to watch her friend's back and try to contain her own thoughts. As well as her laughter.

Oh my goodness. You would think that we had left for a week long trek through the mountains. She can be so testy. One step forward, two steps back. This weekend may not bring us one bit closer than the last hiking weekend.

When Jo returned, Gina had removed all the snacks and had them laying out beside the backpacks.

"We've got two beef jerky sticks, one pack of Twinkies, a bag of Doritos, a pack of peanut butter crackers and three cheese sticks. The only thing I'm wondering is how smashed the Doritos are." She grinned at Jo.

Jo's cigarette and time alone had allowed her to calm herself. And even she was surprised when she returned Gina's smile.

"Well, I guess it's going to have to be the 'lunch of champions' for us. How do you wanna split it?

"Wow, the mountain air is good for you, Jo. You're not even still that bright red color you were a few minutes ago. I'm impressed."

"Don't be. I'm learning that I'm going to have to be the brains of the operation. If we're going to continue to be friends, and I don't kill you on some mountain top, I will need to be in charge of planning. Not you."

"Gee, such kind words, my friend. I can't thank you enough for your confidence in my abilities."

Although the comments dripped with sarcasm, there was laughter from them both. They seemed to be making progress, if not forever, at least for the moment.

The two women took their time with the 'snack lunch'. They conversed and enjoyed the view, even taking the time to make pictures.

Gina thought they should put together a scrapbook of their weekend hikes. Sort of like they did as teenagers.

"Oh, Jo. This conversation reminds me. I've got a scrapbook that I need to give you. I was going to wait til we were with Miss Maureen, because she did help me with it, but looks like that's never going to happen."

"What scrapbook?"

"It's something we put together for you while you were gone. We put it together a long time ago. Probably ten or so years ago. I'll show it to you when we get home. Just don't let me forget."

"Alright. I'll put it with the letters mom gave me a couple of weeks ago. Maybe over the next few years, we can decide how to put it all together and save it for..."

Jo stopped mid-sentence. *Who was she going to save it for?*

"I know what you were gonna say. And I also know you just realized you don't have anyone that readily comes to mind. But you really do. You've got Millie and Jax, and Austin, Ethan, and Hagen. They'll want to learn all about their Aunt Jo one of these days."

"Why Gina? Why would they want to look at stuff, or read anything about someone they don't know? Never really even talked to that much. Why would they want to know?"

"Well, now that you're back home, you can spend some time with all of them. You need to get to know them and they need to get to know you. There's still plenty of time. And trust me, they will want stuff like scrapbooks and letters one day."

They had finished with their lunch and were rested. Time now for the trek back down the bluff.

"This will be so much easier than coming up. It's downhill all the way."

"Some of it is *really* downhill though, Gina. We'll still have to stop and rest. What time is it now?"

"It's almost 1. We should be back by at least 4 or 5. I'll call Millie and tell her we're gonna pass on supper tonight. Tomorrow we're not hiking and we'll have time to eat with them and shoot fireworks."

"Yeah, that is the better plan. When I get back, all I want is a hot shower and a place to sit crash. Oh, and most definitely a glass or two of nice, cold, chardonnay."

The descent down the bluff really did turn out to be much easier than the climb up, even for Jo. The views on the way down had lost some of their awe for Jo; possibly because she had already seen them once, or because it was well over ninety degrees by the time they made their way down. Or because she was simply too exhausted to care. Either way, she wasn't as enamored with the beauty of the mountains coming down as she had been going up.

Conversation was sparse as each woman concentrated on keeping their footing on the steep mountain trail and they really just didn't feel much like talking. Tired at fifty-something, especially if you're hiking, means that you simply keep your mouth shut and walk!

"Oh, thank God! I see the cabin." It was Jo that broke the silence of the last hour or so.

"Yep, there she is – such a beautiful sight today. Much better than yesterday. She doesn't even look old and run down today!" Gina giggled.

"I'm on my last leg. This ole girl is headed for the showers and hot food! You wanna flip for the first one in the shower?"

"Naw, you go ahead. I'm gonna call Millie and tell her we're not coming over for supper tonight. I'll pop one of those frozen lasagnas I packed in the oven and we'll have lasagna and Chardonnay for supper. Sound good to you?"

"That sounds heavenly! I can't wait to get in that shower. Man, I never thought I'd be so thankful for hot water and a bath! Maybe it'll help with these tired, sore muscles, too."

As they hit the cleared area surrounding the cabin, Jo began removing the backpack, unloading the weight and the weariness of the hike.

By the time she reached the cabin, she was down to removing hiking boots and clothes. Ready for the hot shower that she had almost turned into a moment of worship.

As they threw the gear on the front porch, and opened the cabin door, suffocating heat burst forth from the cabin.

"Oh, no. I forgot that we needed to raise the windows before we left. The tin from the roof will have turned this place into a sauna by now."

And sure enough, it was really close.

"I don't care. I don't care. Give me a hot shower, and I can deal with anything." Jo mumbled as she entered the cabin door.

As she headed for the bathroom, she heard Gina speak, but was honestly too tired to care.

I'll ask her what she said when I get out.

The shower area had been one of the upgrades to the cabin, and since it was basically an afterthought, was located at the very back of the cabin. Basically, they had cut out a doorway on the back wall of the cabin, added a small room and moved on to the next repairs. The room that held the shower was only a small four foot by four foot area. Just large enough for a shower stall and room to dress and undress.

Boy, they didn't waste any money on extras with this cabin. Just the bare necessities here. I don't care – it runs clean, hot water, and that's all I need.

Jo turned the shower knobs as she started to remove clothing.

Yes! Thank you God, for letting me make it back to this wonderful little luxury!

She stuck her hand in the shower to test the temperature of the water. It was cold.

Mmm… ok, I'll turn the cold water off and start with only hot.

She turned the hot water to wide open. Still cold.

Mmm… I guess it needs a few more minutes…

She busied herself picking up crumpled, sweaty clothes and folding them for the journey home.

All the while, eyeing the shower for the steam that would indicate hot water. Nothing. Once more she stuck her hand to the water. Still ice cold.

Jesus! Please tell me we have hot water.

She wrapped the towel around her like a robe and opened the door to the cabin.

"Gina! Gina! Where are you?"

"Right here, what's wrong?"

"There's no hot water. It was hot last night. Can you check the water heater, please?"

"Sure, but its outside at the back of the cabin. Give me just a minute. I'll be right back."

"Well don't worry. I'll be right here. Not going anywhere wrapped in a towel." Jo could already sense her grip on calm was slipping.

Please, please let it work. I really, really need a hot bath.

Gina returned in a few minutes.

"Well, I found the water heater, and everything seems fine. I hit the reset on it. Try the hot water now."

Jo returned to the shower stall and turned the hot water knob. After a minute or so, the water was still ice cold.

Gina had stationed herself at the door, and although it was closed, hollered to Jo.

"Well?"

"Not one damn drop of hot water. You gotta be kiddin' me!"

"I guess there may be something wrong with the elements. It is an old water heater and probably hasn't been checked at all this year."

"Well that don't help one little bit right now, does it?"

It was all Jo could do not to explode. Even as she took the coldest shower she thought she had taken in all her life, it did nothing to abate the heat of anger surging through her body.

All I wanted was a nice, hot shower...

As she emerged from the shower room, Gina was riffling through her things, looking for her Oil of Olay.

"Jo, don't you use Oil of Olay? Did you bring yours?"

It was more than Jo could take.

"Seriously, Gina, you want to know, in the middle of this ridiculously old, no-hot-water, snake infested pit that we're going to call a 'cabin in the woods' if I brought any Oil of Olay?"

At that moment, and in the blink of an eye, two old friends eyed each other warily. Warily and with a certain steel resolve. There were vast expanses of difference that threatened at any moment to boil over and explode into violent words. Except for a tremendous amount of discipline and the perfectly timed hair raising scream, it probably wouldn't have ended in the comical way that it did. Once again, however, fate reminded them of the ties that bound them together. Whether it be because of their shared experiences, beliefs, or the simple need to survive. This time, it was the need to survive. The question about the Oil of Olay, and the unleashing of harsh words, erased in the exact moment they heard the blood curdling scream.

CHAPTER 14

I wish I felt this way at home....
Yes, I wish I felt this way at home.

Dolly Parton

BOTH WOMEN JUMPED AS though they'd been shot. Gina was the first to recover.

"What the hell was that?"

"How do I know? You're the mountain woman. You tell me. It sounded like someone screaming bloody murder."

Night had fallen during their efforts to shower, change, and cook and it was impossible to discern what it was or where the sound had originated.

Neither woman was willing to open the front door, and so stood peering like mice from the window.

"I'm gonna get my gun."

"Why? You can't see anything to shoot. And my God, if it's a person, please don't shoot!"

"Well, what are we gonna do? Just sit here and wait?"

"You got a better idea?"

As they peered from the window and contemplated their options, flashlights appeared at the edge of the clearing.

"Oh, God, Gina. We're going to die. I bet whoever that is, they know what that noise was. Hell, it might even have been one of them. I'm gettin' the gun."

At this point Gina could make out four figures – two adults and two kids.

"No, you're not. They've got two kids with them. Calm down."

Finally, the four figures came close enough for Gina to see that it was Millie, David and the kids.

"See, I told you. Leave the damn gun in the bag. It's David, Millie, and the girls."

Gina flung open the cabin door, and rushed to greet them all, at once asking for answers to the blood-curdling scream they'd heard.

"David, what in the world was that screaming sound?"

David began to laugh.

"I can see that it scared you almost as much as it scared the girls, here. It was a bobcat. I thought I was gonna have to muzzle Bella and Henley. I'm surprised you didn't hear them scream."

"Well, we might've if we hadn't been so startled and scared to death ourselves." Gina stooped to hug the girls and assure them they weren't the only ones that had been afraid.

"You two might've warned us that there was a bobcat around here." She looked pointedly at David and Millie.

"Well, Mom, it's not like they're not in these mountains all the time anyway. Good heavens, I figured you would already know that."

"They may be, but I've never heard a sound like that in my entire life. It was just like a woman screaming for her life."

"You're a scaredy-cat now. You're getting old and scared of everything."

It was David that seemed to be making fun of Gina's age as well as her disposition at this point in her life.

"Mmph..." Was all he got in reply.

"What are ya'll doin' over here anyway?"

"The girls wanted to come see you and Aunt Jo, so we decided an evening stroll might be a good idea. Apparently, it was a good idea for everyone. I'd hate for you two to spend the night holed up like scared mice."

Jo and Gina glanced at each other. If not for the scream and the visit from Millie and David, they might be involved in their own screaming match, behaving like anything but mice.

The visit turned out to be quite pleasant and David determined that the elements in the water heater were burned out. Gina was forced to shower with cold water as well, but he left with a promise to send someone out to complete the necessary repairs the next day.

By the time the visit was over, so was most of the night. It was a tired and bedraggled Jo and Gina that turned in for the night; too tired to even begin to want to pick up their disagreement at the late hour.

Besides, morning might bring a fresh perspective.

The morning of the 4th of July, 2012 dawned and a beautiful day seemed sure to follow. Jo hadn't bothered to set her usual 5:30 alarm, and neither woman stirred before 8 o'clock.

It was actually Gina that was the first to wake.

"Jo, Jo, you awake?"

"I am now." Was all that she got in reply.

"I'm getting' up to make some coffee. C'mon, it's after 8 o'clock. We need to get up."

"Why? I AM NOT hiking again today. It may take me thirty minutes just to get out of this bed. Good lord, my body doesn't want to work!"

She heard Gina chuckle.

"It's not funny. Aren't you sore from yesterday? Please tell me your legs are hurtin' as bad as mine."

"Nope. Not really. I can tell they're a little overused from yesterday, but I'm not really that sore."

"I can't live your life. Your body is more accustomed to this shit than mine. I like my nice, soft office chair. My treadmill and my wonderful HOT shower."

"Aww, c'mon Jo. You're fine. You'll be good as new after coffee and breakfast. C'mon, coffee's ready now."

They grabbed their mugs of steaming-hot-life-in-a-cup and headed for the front porch.

"Well, these chairs may not be as nice as office chairs, but they're pretty comfy."

Jo had to admit they were comfortable. Someone had taken the time to fit each of the porch chairs with plump, cushy pillow-like coverings.

"They're not bad. Whatever they're stuffed with, they're really soft."

As they sipped their coffee, they watched the daily activity of the mountain come to life. Slowly, they came to life as well.

"Jo, do you want to talk about last night?"

"No, I wanna forget that I lost my temper and got so completely pissed off about something as stupid as a hot shower. I was so tired, and honestly, big doses of hiking and your way of doin'g things drives me insane. It's not your fault, and it's not my fault. It simply is what it is."

"If it's any consolation, I would probably be in the same boat, had I moved to Washington, DC to live and try to integrate into your lifestyle. I don't think our issue is each other so much as it is the fact you're trying to adjust to a new way of life."

"I suppose you're right about that part. When you throw in the fact that I'm worried about mom, you and I have spent a lifetime apart, and I think I'm overwhelmed. The easiest thing to do is take it out on you. I'm sorry about yesterday, Gina. Let's forget it and move on."

"Excellent choice, my friend. What do you say we go visit Max and Maxine today, have a nice hot meal prepared by someone else and look forward to the fireworks tonight?"

Jo rolled her eyes. Then smiled.

"I'm not even gonna let ole 'Max the Misfit' get me down today. Fine, let's go visit and most importantly, let's have a hot meal at a real table!"

They finished their coffee and Gina went inside to throw together a cheese toast. No sense in a heavy breakfast if they were going to eat lunch at the store. They were soon dressed and ready for the road.

The short walk from the cabin to the jeep did wonders for Jo's legs, and by the time she climbed in to drive, most of the soreness was gone.

"I need to call Stella today. Mom's been there since Sunday, and I really want to make sure she's having a good time. She was a little reluctant to go when Stella came to get her. I'm not really sure if she didn't want to go anywhere, or she didn't want to go to Stella's."

"Well, here, let me drive and you give her a call on the way to the store. Swap places with me."

Jo swapped places with Gina and picked up her phone to call her sister.

"Oh, my God. Something must be wrong. I've got 8 voicemail messages from Stella. Shit."

As she punched the button on her phone labeled Stella, Gina cranked the jeep and pulled out of the parking area. At least they would have service all the way to the store.

The phone rang only once before Stella picked up on the other end.

"Thank God you finally called. You can't imagine what a time I've had with Mom these last couple of days. Jo, she's losing her mind. I mean completely losing her mind."

"Well slow down, Stella. What's happened? What has she done?"

"First, and the biggest issue, is completely losing her in the mall. I mean, just losing her. I couldn't find her anywhere. I took her with me to stop by and check on the Arcade, Jack's had to work and needed me to see about things. I told her when we got there, to wait on me right outside. They had a nice bench she could sit on and wait for a few minutes. Jo, I wasn't gone 10 minutes, and when I came out – no Mom. I walked up and down the mall, several times. I checked the bathrooms, I checked the food court – nothing. She had just vanished. Well, she won't carry a cell phone, so you don't have any way to call her. Hell, at this point, I doubt she'd even know what a phone was, much less answer it. Anyway, I finally alerted the mall security; you wanna guess where we found her? She was walking around outside, at the BACK of the mall. Walking around aimlessly, mumbling something about looking for Tom."

At that, a breathless Stella stopped long enough for Jo to jump into the conversation.

"I told you something was wrong. I've been trying to tell you this for months now. Mom has something wrong. She's not just getting' old and forgetful. Something else is happening. I am pretty certain she has Alzheimer's, Stella."

"Well, we've got to have something done. I mean, I can't deal with this, on top of a husband and kids that are driving me nuts. I need a break myself; I can't handle something like this when Mom comes to visit, Jo. I just can't."

"Look Stella, I'm in the middle of the Ozark Mountains. I can't do anything right this minute, but if you'll handle it til tomorrow, I'll be back. When are you bringing her home, tomorrow afternoon?"

"Yes, at least by tomorrow afternoon. It may be tomorrow

morning. I've got some things to see about for Jack tomorrow, too. It looks like I can't leave Mom alone, so I may just bring her home tomorrow morning. What time will you be back? Don't you think she'll be alright once I get her home?"

"How do I know? I had no idea she would just wander off like that. I haven't had this issue with her at home. It's possible that it's so bad right now because she's in unfamiliar surroundings. I should be home by at least 3 or 4 in the afternoon. Just bring her as late as you can tomorrow morning, then I'll go by there as soon as I get home."

"Alright, but Jo we've got to do something. She can't come back up here like this. She just can't. She'll wander off into God knows what, and we'll never find her."

"I know, Stella. Just see about her til in the morning. We'll deal with it when I get home."

A distressed and disgusted Jo hung up the phone.

"Good gracious! You would think I had asked Stella to have another baby. I tried to tell her something was wrong with Mom, and she wouldn't listen. Now she can see for herself."

Jo relayed the parts of the conversation that Gina couldn't hear on the final leg of the trip to the store.

"She's got Alzheimer's, Jo. That's exactly what's wrong with her. Even if you don't have a family history that is what's wrong. And besides, up until the last few decades, doctors never diagnosed the behavior. They thought people got old, ornery, and forgetful. You probably wouldn't know if your grandparents had it because they didn't diagnose it back then."

"Well, we've got to do something. She can't be left alone much longer or she's gonna get herself in a world of trouble and not even realize it."

They pulled into the parking lot.

"Speaking of a world of trouble, I wonder how Max and Maxine are doin'? Surely they've made up by now. For our sake, and all those customers too!"

Gina laughed. She really did hope the storm had passed.

Things were bustling as usual inside the small country store, and Jo and Gina made their way to an empty table.

"I don't care what comes or goes today, I want to see Lucy and order our lunch. The rest I can deal with as it comes."

Gina nodded to confirm her agreement and began to look for Lucy. She spotted her on the other side of the store and waved to signal they desperately needed her attention.

Lucy was happy to oblige.

"Hey ladies. Glad to see Hemmed In Hollow didn't kill ya. Ready for lunch?"

"More than ready. I'll have whatever is hot and you recommend. Oh, and a nice big glass of sweet tea, please."

"What about you Gina? What do you want?"

"The same thing. We're not hard to please today. We forgot to pack food for lunch yesterday, and that lasagna I attempted to fix last night, was sorely lacking in 'great taste'. Just bring on a hot meal!"

Lucy didn't even try to hide her laughter. "Got it, hiking and camping isn't everything it's cracked up to be. Hot food on the way! Oh, and I'll let Maxine know you're here. Max is out back with the smoker, but Maxine's in the kitchen. Thank you so much for whatever you said or did the other day. They've been like newlyweds ever since."

"Nothing like a little friendly advice and a near-death experience to bring out the best in people," Gina replied, as Lucy was making her way to the kitchen.

She glanced around the room and her gaze stopped on a man standing at the counter.

"Hey, there's Aaron. You didn't get to meet him last time you were here. Let me call him over so I can introduce you two."

An excited Gina got up to go bring Aaron over to the table, about the same time Lucy returned with their tea.

"Jo, meet Aaron Hall; Aaron, meet Jo Felsenthal. I wanted to introduce you two the last time we were here, but you had gone somewhere and we missed you."

"Hello, Jo." Said a deep voice that just didn't seem to fit the slight-of-build man that stood before her. "Very nice to meet you. And no, I wasn't here a few weeks ago. I had business elsewhere", as he glanced at Lucy.

Gina seemed oblivious to the look that had passed between them. She went on to explain to Jo once again that Aaron was a permanent resident, an electrician and helped Max with the electrical issues that come from running a store. Especially a store with cabins and an RV Park.

"Well, Aaron, it's very nice to meet you. I look forward to seeing you on future visits to this beautiful place. I think Gina loves it more than she does her own home."

"It wouldn't be the first time someone fell in love with these mountains. I was so smitten I moved here permanently. I can understand how that happens. Well, nice visiting with you ladies, but I've got to get started on the list Max has for me. That's what happens when you leave for a couple of weeks; your 'to do' list becomes a book! See you later."

Lucy was returning with two plates as Aaron made his way from the table. No time for talk now. Food was arriving!

As they dove into the first hot meal that they could really enjoy in two days, conversation and even the activity of the store took a back seat.

"God, that was good!" Jo finally stopped long enough to comment.

"I may not agree with Max and his views on the government, but they can sure put out great food!"

"You ain't kiddin'. I think that was the best BBQ I've ever had." Gina grinned. "Of course it doesn't help that we haven't had a hot meal in two days."

Lucy returned to refill their tea glasses, about the time Max emerged from the kitchen.

"Uh-oh. Here we go." Jo almost whispered.

"Hello, ladies. Back again, I see. Just couldn't stay away from the good food, uh?"

"Actually, Max, it's your company that we crave!" Gina replied.

"Yeah right. Like I crave a heart cath."

"Oh, does this mean you've have an appointment with a doctor?"

"Yes, that means I have an appointment. You know how that old woman is back there, once she sinks her teeth into something, she won't let go. She called the doctor, made the appointment, and now she's determined to go with me for the visit." Max stopped long enough to roll his eyes in exasperation. "Like I'm not gonna go and tell him everything unless she's there to witness it?"

"You probably wouldn't. She understands you as well as I do."

He flashed Gina a mischievous grin and turned to look at Jo. "Women, you just can't get around'em."

"How are you today, Miss Jo? Ready to finish our conversation?"

"I don't know if I'm ready for another round with you or not, Max. I'm havin' a really good day and I don't want to be forced to think about anything too much."

"Well, you might be interested in this piece of information. I actually had a conversation with my son, you know, the one you think so highly of… anyway, he tells me he's coming for a visit Labor Day weekend. Would you have anything to do with this?"

"Maybe… I really miss George and Maggie. I can't go to

Washington because of my Mom, but I've coerced them into comin'g here. He didn't tell me you had talked to him though."

"Maggie? Who's Maggie?"

"Maggie is another friend of mine and she and George work together. They're both comin'g for a visit at the same time."

"Mmm…. sounds like George and Maggie are a 'George and Maggie' couple to me."

"I don't think so. And anyway, I wouldn't read too much into them comin'g at the same time. I invited them to come at the same time."

"I'm sure you did. It's just that they didn't have to accept your invitation at the same time."

"Well, anyway. I didn't realize they were comin'g up here, too. When did you talk to him?"

"Yesterday. I only called because Maxine wouldn't shut up until I called him and asked him to come here – she thinks I'm fixin' to die, apparently."

"Oh, Max," Gina interjected, "she just wants you to be on the best terms possible with your children, regardless of what's not going to happen."

"Well, anyway, when George and Maggie come for a visit, I'd like to visit with you two ladies as well. Gina, you come as close to a daughter as I've ever known, and I'd like to have you all here at the same time. Please?"

Jo's view of Max softened at that moment. She never dreamed the man even knew the word 'please', much less used it.

"Yes, of course, Max. We'd love to come and visit at the same time. You just reserve us a cabin, and we'll be here."

Gina never stopped to even look at Jo or ask her thoughts. She was too afraid the answer might be 'no'.

Jo kicked her under the table, as if to say, 'hey, what about my thoughts?' Too late.

"And Jo, I don't want you to leave today without some further information on my position about the government. I don't want you to misunderstand: Our Constitution makes it clear that we need governance. My issue lies with *how much* governance we need. There was a time that the Federal Government operated within the intended scope of the Constitution. Today, thanks to all the technology available, and some very liberal, progressive members of the government system, they've over stepped their bounds. *That*, is what I take issue with."

"Well, Max, the government is trying to protect us. Protect us from all the bad things and bad people that exist in the world today."

"There's something you don't understand here, Jo. What if we don't want our precious government to save us from ourselves… maybe we like having the chance to decide…even if we're wrong. Have you ever thought about that? Perhaps we need the freedom to make bad decisions, just like we need the freedom to make good ones. Freedom is a heady drug, in some sense of the word. Freedom allows for individual choice. Not everybody makes a good choice. But as our forefathers laid out for us, we have God-given rights, and freedom is one of those rights. Our government is taking all that away. They're taking it in the name of protecting us, but they're taking away freedoms and turning us into something that resembles a collective, not an individually free, society. A place where there is no freedom of expression, no freedom. I don't see that as a good thing."

"Max, you're gonna have to give me time to think about this. I don't have a ready answer, with you or against you at this point. I've got too many other issues that require my attention. Arguing for or against government intervention isn't high on my priority right now. But, I promise you this: we will continue this conversation. Because right or wrong, I stand by what I did as a civil servant and in what George continues to do. Ok?"

"Fair enough. Besides, I need to see the doctor and make sure I'll be around long enough to continue this argument with you and George at a later date."

At that moment, Maxine called to Max from the back of the store, and he excused himself, leaving them with a grin and a heartfelt goodbye.

"Well, that was interesting," Gina commented. "You two didn't even seem to be enemies during this conversation."

"I'm just not up to arguing with an old man that looks so comical and apparently has heart issues. Heartless, I am not, Gina."

"Alright, c'mon, let's head back over to the cabin and get ready to shoot fireworks with my awesome grandbabies. Jo, you might even enjoy this part of the holiday!"

Laughing, and in one of the best moods of the trip, they made their way first to the jeep, then back to the cabin.

Changes, they were a takin' place.

CHAPTER 15

Rocky mountain music fills my memory…
Rocky mountain music, can I hear you playing for me?
Eddie Rabbit

THAT NIGHT, WITH THE fireworks and the little girls that were in such awe of the sparkling explosions high above them, Jo and Gina spent one of their finer moments. No one was out of sorts, the happiness from Bella and Henley seemed to overflow and creep into Jo and Gina. When it was all over, they walked the short distance back to the cabin.

"That was truly fun, Gina. I am going to miss being a grandmother, I can tell from one night of watching you with yours."

"Well, I guess you could be an adopted grandmother, of sorts."

"Or I could spend more time with my nephews. They're losing their grandmother as they know her, and could probably use someone to step in and fill her role."

"I swear, Jo. You're becomin'g motherly, even."

"Don't get carried away, Gina. Just because I sense a need to get to know my nephews a little better, doesn't mean I'm becomin'g motherly."

"Whatever you say, Jo. Whatever makes you feel good about it."

They had reached the clearing for their cabin and the conversation turned to packing and preparing to leave in the morning.

"You want me to set my alarm tonight?"

"Sure. Asking you to not set it for two mornings in a row, would be asking too much. Set it and we'll get an early start. I know you really need to get home and check on Miss Maureen anyway."

"I do, and thanks for bein' so understanding. I really need to get home and try to figure out what's got to be done. I don't want her to be dropped off and left alone for very long."

"Yeah, and knowing Stella, that's exactly what she'll do. Once she gets her home, she'll assume Mom will be alright and leave."

"You're right. If she got that turned around in the mall, there's no tellin' what she'll do when she gets home."

"Alright. Let's get ready for bed and a trip home tomorrow."

The next few hours they spent packing and readying themselves to go home. It had been an enlightening holiday.

The next morning, the alarm rang at exactly 5:30 am. Rise and shine and head home.

"Alright, let's head out. Got everything packed?"

"Yep. I'm ready to go. We'll stop and get breakfast on the ride home. Did you tell Millie we were leaving this early? What about the key to the cabin?"

"Yes, I told her. We can drop the key off on our way out. I'm ready, let's go."

They walked the short distance to the jeep and left as the sun began to peek over the horizon.

"How beautiful. People that never experience a sunrise like this have no idea what they're missing. It's so surreal it seems spiritual."

"You know, Gina, if nothing else, my time with you reminds me of how much I have to be thankful for. Thank you, friend for reminding me that we do have a lot to appreciate."

Gina hopped out at the registration post and dropped the key.

The return trip home was as beautiful as the trip up had been and they spent the next several hours in conversation and comradery. It was with regret that they reached Jo's cabin and parted ways.

"Well, I can say that this time I truly enjoyed our journey, Gina. You wanna give me a call on Saturday? We're missing our usual Thursday coffee meeting, so why don't we get together Saturday morning?"

"Yeah, I'll call, and if you need me when you check Miss Maureen, you call me. Thanks, Jo. This was a really special trip. I'll talk to you on Saturday."

Jo watched as Gina disappeared down the drive. Paul had been right, they needed time to learn each other all over again, but it seemed there was hope for common ground.

As she unlocked the door to her cabin, the familiar smells of home assailed her.

Oh, how wonderful to be home. I had a great time, but it's so good to come home. Wow! What a difference a few months makes. Imagine me having these thoughts about Polk Ridge again. Funny how things sneak up on you.

The ringing cell phone pulled her from her thoughts.

"Hey, Mom. Are you home? I just got back. I thought I might run over and check on things as soon as I get unpacked."

It was a quite shaky Maureen that answered her daughter's questions.

"Yeah, Jo. Stella brought me home a few hours ago, but I really want to see you. Please come when you get through with your unpacking. Do you mind pickin' us up something for lunch? I don't feel like doin' anything at the moment. That trip to Stella's was really hard. I wanna talk to you. Please c'mon as soon as you can."

"I will. In fact, I'll just wait about unpacking. I can stop by the diner and pick up some lunch. I should be there in about an hour. Love you, Mom. Be there in a bit."

"Love you too. Bye Jo."

Miss Maureen's shaky voice unnerved Jo more than she cared to admit.

This is spiraling out of control. Mom sounded so lonely, so out of sorts. We may have to address this sooner than I thought.

She pulled herself out of her thoughts and headed for the jeep. It wouldn't take long to pick up lunch and get there.

As she drove down the driveway she had spent most of her life travelling, she really took a good look this time. So many things were in disrepair. So much had been let go over the last few years. This place needed help. Her mom needed help. She just wasn't sure what to do. Nor was she sure she had all the answers.

"Hey Mom. I got us lunch."

Maureen was in the kitchen and the house was as hot as a blistering summer day.

"What are you doin'?"

"I'm fixin us a bite to eat. I turned the stove on to let it heat up, and then I'm gonna cook this chicken pie I'm workin' on. What have you got there?"

Jo had grabbed the bags from the jeep and was standing in the kitchen doorway, bags still in hand.

"Well, Momma you said to pick up something for lunch. So I stopped by the diner. Don't you remember?"

Miss Maureen's face spoke volumes. The crushed, tearful expression told Jo more than words could have ever expressed.

"Jo, something is so wrong with me. I truly don't know what to do." The words came tumbling from her mom as fast as a flowing river.

"I got lost at the mall with Stella, she was so mad, I don't know what happened. I don't even know why I wound up at the back of the mall. I've become so stupid."

She was in tears by the time she finished, right along with Jo.

"Momma, don't worry. We'll figure this out. We'll go talk with a doctor and try to figure out what's wrong. Reckon you're just becomin'g a little more forgetful? I don't know, I just don't know. But we'll figure it out together. I tell you what, no more trips to Stella's or anywhere else til we know what's wrong. I'll come stay with you til we can get a doctor's appointment and figure out what we need to do, ok?"

"Oh, Jo. I hate to turn your life upside down just because mine's in such disarray. I don't know what to do… I've never been so lost. My thoughts have never been so jumbled. I wish your daddy was still here. He'd know exactly what to do; he could fix this."

"Perhaps, Mom. But since he's not, we'll fix it together, ok?"

Inside, Jo knew that with or without Tom Felsenthal, this was going to be a hard journey. She was convinced that her mom was suffering from a disease for which there was no cure. There was no fix.

I need Gina. I need to talk to Paul. And I need to talk to my sister. My mom needs me. How does life continue to be more complicated than ever? I thought it would be so simple by now.

"Here, I've got lunch. Sit down and let's eat and visit."

Jo fixed them some tea, turned off the stove, ignored whatever it was that her mom thought was chicken pie and sat down to eat and talk with her Mom.

Troubles be dammed. I'm just gonna be my momma's daughter for the next thirty minutes.

They ate and talked. They laughed and spent time recalling old memories. They were mother and daughter and they simply took time to enjoy each other.

When they finished with lunch, and Jo began to clear the table, Miss Maureen got up from her chair.

"Jo, honey I'm going upstairs and take a bath. I'm tired from my visit with Stella, and I only wanna get a bath and take a nap."

"That's fine, Mom. Go ahead. I'll clean up. I need to make a few phone calls, run home and get some clothes, and then I'll come back and spend the night. Ok?"

"Ok. Are you sure it's not too much trouble? I hate to put you kids out. I don't want to be a troublesome old woman."

"You're not a troublesome old woman. I don't mind one bit. Go on and take a shower and then a nap. I'll be right here cleaning up. I'll stay til you wake up, then I'll run home and get some clothes. Go on."

Jo shooed her mother on upstairs and set about to clean up the kitchen. It was in complete disarray. Whatever Maureen had begun to cook wound up at the end of the yard for the animals to figure out.

Finally, Jo finished in the kitchen and went out to the front porch to smoke and call Gina. Jo didn't even bother with hello.

"Gina, I'm at Mom's. She was a total mess after that trip to Stella's. She called as soon as I walked in the door at home. This is worse than I thought. Is there a doctor around here that can give her whatever she needs to determine if she has Alzheimer's or do I need to take her to Little Rock?"

"Jo, there's not really anybody here except our general practitioner. She really needs somebody that knows the disease and how to treat it. Let me make a few phone calls. I'll try to find a good doctor, but you'll probably have to go to Little Rock. I'll call you back tomorrow afternoon. Til then, you need any help? Need anything?"

"No. I'm going to get clothes and come stay with her til we can figure out what to do. Thank God I didn't sign up to teach a summer class. Now, there's no reason I can't stay with her for the next month or so, anyway. Alright, just call me tomorrow when you find out something, and Gina, thanks."

"No need to thank me. What are friends for?"

Jo hung up the phone relieved that she had Gina's help.

Thank God she can help me. If not for her, I wouldn't have a clue who to call. I haven't even been to a doctor here, much less have any idea about a good specialist. Note to self: Ask mom who her regular doctor is.

It was almost 4 by now, and the afternoon shadows were beginning to gather. Jo still loved her childhood home. The front porch, the woods that surrounded them. She hadn't been to her secret place since her dad died. Now would be a great opportunity to calm herself and spend some time alone.

She stepped off the porch and headed for the creek bank that ran along the right side of the house. It was so shallow you could simply hop across it. It only took her eyes a minute to adjust in the shadows of the old oak trees, and there it was. Still beckoning her to find shelter in the vines and leaves that made it one of the best hiding places she'd ever found.

As she plopped down on the dirt, she realized how tired she was. How sad she was. And for the moment, how confused she was about her mother. The tears flowed slowly at first, then with all the fierceness of a rushing river.

How did I get here? So old and all alone. No family. No husband. No one to lean on. Not so long ago, I felt as if I could conquer the world. When did that leave me? Now, all I want is to hide in someone's arms. Lean on someone stronger than me.

As the tears subsided, so did the sensation of utter loneliness.

Stop feeling sorry for yourself. You've got a mother in that house that needs you more than ever. You're not alone. You have family – granted not your own, but still family. And you've got some great friends. Shake it off, Jo.

She rose and forced herself back towards the house. Mom should be awake by now. I need to run get clothes. I need to at least unpack and get back over here before it's very late.

As she crossed the yard, the faint sound of Miss Maureen calling her drifted to her ears.

"I'm here mom, outside. I'm coming."

Maureen met her at the door.

"Oh, ok honey. You weren't inside and I wanted to tell you I'm so much better after the nap. You don't have to come stay with me. I'll be fine. I promise."

"Mom, that's not a good idea. At least let me come and stay to-night. After tonight, we'll re-evalute. I need to be here for a few days, anyway. You seemed pretty shaken up while ago."

"I know I did. But honestly, I really do feel better. Being at home helps so much. Stella's house is so different, and all they do is so different to my day. I'll be much better now."

"Well, I guess so. But I'm comin'g back tonight anyway. I'm gonna run home now and unpack, gather up some clothes for tomorrow and I should be back by 7, ok?"

"Alright, Jo. Evidently I'm not gonna talk you out of this. I'll be in the living room watching TV. I'll be there you when you get back." She turned to go inside.

Jo stopped her just shy of the door.

"Mom, I love you. I'm really tryin' to do what's best for you and me." She hugged her for a long few minutes.

"I know honey. Now, shoo, go on and get your stuff."

On the trip home she called Stella. No answer.

I'll try her again on the way back.

As she reached the cabin, her phone rang.

"Paul, hey. I wasn't expecting a call from you. How was your 4th of July?"

Hey, Jo. Rather dull. How'd the campin' trip with Gina go? You two make any progress at tryin' to understand each other?"

There was definite laughter in his voice. He knew enough about each of them to know the camping trip had most likely turned into some kind of adventure.

"Actually, we had a great time. I didn't strangle her. She didn't throw anything at me. Although, at the very beginning of the hike, we had some pretty rough moments." It was Jo's turn for laughter.

She spent the next thirty minutes or so unpacking, then repacking for her night with Miss Maureen and relaying the last few days events.

As she got ready to go, it was Paul that interrupted.

"Jo, before you hang up, you know if you need anything, anything at all, all you have to do is call. Your mom means a lot to me too. I want to help if I can."

There was so much sincerity in his voice that Jo almost teared up.

"Thanks, Paul. You don't know how much I do appreciate the concern and your offer of help. There are moments where I'm so overwhelmed and really don't know what I need to do. I will call, I promise. If for nothing more than the comfort of a kind voice on the other end."

He was silent for a long few seconds. Jo thought they'd lost connection.

"Paul, you still there?"

"Yes, I'm still here. Take care of yourself, Jo. I'll make a point of comin'g by to visit Miss Maureen when I get home in September. Til then, call me if you need me. Bye."

An exhausted but peaceful Jo made her way back to her Mom's. Talking to Paul really did seem to make it better.

The next morning, Jo woke at her usual 5:30. There weren't any other sounds comin'g from the house.

Mom must still be asleep. I'll go make some coffee then check on her.

Jo quietly made coffee, then padded upstairs to peep in on her Mom. She was still sleeping.

Her face seemed so peaceful. Who could guess there might be something wrong inside that beautiful head?

She turned to go, and at that moment, Maureen called out to her daughter.

"I see you peeping in the door. I'm forgetful, not infirmed. I smell coffee, too. I'll be on down in just a minute."

Jo smiled as she descended the stairs. Forgetful or not, she still had a sense of humor.

They spent the morning tidying the house and cleaning. It seemed to Jo her mom could sure manage to make a mess in a relatively short time. She had cleaned before she left with Gina last weekend.

Finally, they were finished, and stopped for lunch.

"Ok, Mom. What'll it be? Turkey sandwiches or ham?"

"Neither. I don't have either one of those in the fridge. I need to go grocery shopping. You wanna go with me? Afraid I'll forget where the Shop-n-Save's at?" She grinned at Jo.

"Well, you seem much better today! But, yes I'd like to go with you. I need a few groceries myself. We can stop and eat lunch while we're in town, then go to the grocery."

The rest of the day seemed to fly by, and as they returned home, Jo realized there had not been one time her Mom had forgotten anything.

"Mom, maybe you are better. We've not had one incident today. You've remembered everything."

"I told you I was better yesterday. You just don't know how unsettling it is for me now to go somewhere like Stella's. It's so different to home. It makes me aggravated, and that's when I start to forget so much."

They unpacked groceries for Miss Maureen, and Jo reluctantly admitted she really did need to go home for a while.

"I know, you've got things at your house you need to tend to. Go on Jo. I'll be fine. I'll even call you right before I go to bed. How about that? Will that make you more at ease?"

"Yes, it would. Ok, I'm going home tonight. But promise you'll call me before you go to bed?"

"Yes, I promise. Bye, sweetheart. Go, now."

On the way home, Jo remembered that she hadn't heard from Gina.

Wonder why she didn't call?

She punched the button to call Gina.

"Hey. You didn't call today, so I thought I'd call you. Did you find out anything about a doctor?"

"Well, yes and no. Yes, I discovered that there's no one here that can run the test that you need. But no, I didn't find a doctor in Little Rock yet. Where are you?"

"On my way home. Mom had a much better day today than yesterday. She insisted that I go home tonight, and I really do need to do a few things at home, so I gave in. I still haven't gotten hold of Stella. I tried her twice yesterday, but no answer. I don't know what the hell she's got goin' on, but she needs to return my calls."

"Well, I'm at home, but I found that scrapbook I wanted to give you. Vicky's supposed to call me back tonight with the name of a doctor for your Mom in Little Rock. You want some company?"

"Sure, I should be home in a few minutes. Just come on when you get ready. I'll be there."

They hung up and Jo was home in less than 10 minutes.

Finally, a chance to sleep in my own bed!

Jo was putting away groceries when she heard Gina's car in the drive.

Wow. That was quick.

She knocked as she reached the front door, but never waited on Jo to answer.

"Hey, you in here?"

"Yeah, c'mon in. I'm puttin' away these groceries I got with Mom today. How about a glass of Chardonnay? And a stint on the front porch?"

"Absolutely!"

Jo popped the cork on the last bottle in the fridge and they took up residence on the porch.

"Well, I gotta say Mom did appear to be much better today. She didn't have one incident of forgetting anything. Perhaps it's not as bad as it seems. It's possible it was simply the trip to Stella's."

"Well, that might be the problem. Especially if she has Alzheimer's. It gets worried when you take them out of their own environment. Vicky called while I was on my way over and gave me the name of a specialist in Little Rock. If I were you, I'd call and make an appointment and let them check her. She may not be too far along, and if not, they can give her some medicine to help with things. There's not a cure, but there is help Jo."

They spent the next half hour exchanging information for the doctor and what little knowledge they had about the disease.

"Ok, now let me run get the scrapbook. You gotta check this out. It's amazing at the information your Mom kept all these years. I'll be right back."

When she returned, with scrapbook in hand, Jo couldn't believe all the newspaper clippings, photos and information Miss Maureen had managed to keep.

"My goodness, I didn't even know they put lots of this in the newspaper. And look at all the postcards! Mom kept everything I ever sent. Even information I didn't send – places I was stationed. She must've spent hours looking up some of this information."

"And so many pictures from high school. Oh my goodness. I really don't want anybody to see some of these. I look so gawky, so silly."

"Well, to your Mom you looked perfect. She and I spent hours putting this thing together. I've had the book for the better part of ten years. Even when the kids were little, we'd visit Miss Maureen, and they would beg for the book with pictures of 'Aunt Jo'. That's one reason they still call you that today. It really does seem like you're a member of the family."

"Why did she give it to you?"

"When Robert died. She thought I needed something to remind me of brighter days. This was the best that she had to share with me. The only thing she made me promise, was to pass it on to you when you came home. Not just for a visit, but when you came home to stay. So, here it is. I hope it'll be as comforting to you as it has been to me."

"Oh, Gina. Thanks for everything. Thanks for being a friend to my mom. Thanks for keeping this safe for so many years. And most of all, thanks for being my friend."

"Don't forget to thank me for draggin' you on these hiking trips. I know how much you've enjoyed all that!"

Gina once again flashed that infectious grin.

"Believe it or not, I really did enjoy this last trip. I can't say that much for the first one; but this last one was great."

They continued to talk and look at the scrapbook til almost nine, and it was Miss Maureen that brought them out of their conversation when Jo's phone rang.

"Hey, Mom. True to your word, uh? Ready for bed?"

"Yes, and I didn't forget to call, either. See? I'm not completely senile yet."

"Apparently not. Ok, go on to bed. I'll call you tomorrow."

As she hung up, Gina was getting up to go home.

"I've got to go, anyway, Jo. It's after nine, and I need to get on home."

"Gina, thanks again for bringin' me the book. I'm gonna put it with all the letters Mom gave me and the journals I've been keeping all these years – who knows? One day we might decide to write a book about all these years. Got any ideas about a name?"

"No, but it should include the words 'insane' or 'nuts' somewhere in the title."

She giggled and reached to hug Jo all at the same time.

"Save those thoughts for another day."

With that, she was gone. And Jo was so ready to call it a day. Time to sink between the sheets in HER bed. Tomorrow was another day.

CHAPTER 16

Stood alone on a mountain top, starin' out at the great divide.
I could go east, I could go west, it was all up to me to decide.
Just then I saw a young hawk flyin'
And my soul began to rise
And pretty soon
My heart was singin'
Roll, roll me away, won't you roll me away tonight

Bob Seger

THE NEXT FEW WEEKS that rolled by for Jo and Gina were nothing but sunshine. But, just as summer comes to a close, so does an uneventful few weeks of respite.

Jo looked up from her computer and realized that it was almost August. She had just received an email that required her to commit to the upcomin'g fall semester of online courses. She was more than a little apprehensive about giving them a positive confirmation.

She had already been to Little Rock with Miss Maureen to see Dr. Willenfield. The test necessary to diagnose Alzheimer's had been done, and they were waiting on the results. There had only been a few episodes with Maureen in the last few weeks, and Jo was beginning to doubt that it was anything but simple old-age dementia.

I suppose it's possible it is only old age. It's possible I'm being too cautious. But what if it's not? Can I see about Mom and make time to teach? Then there's the visit from George and Maggie in September; and thanks to Gina, one more trip to visit with Max and Maxine. Mmmm…

She had made a real effort to spend more time with her Mom but another overnight stay hadn't seemed necessary. She had even tried, unsuccessfully, to involve Stella in the process of finding a doctor and deciding about testing for Alzheimer's.

Several days after returning from the 4th of July holiday with Gina, Jo had finally managed to get Stella on the phone. The ensuing conversation left them with a bigger void in their relationship than had existed before. Jo truly tried to understand Stella's reluctance to admit there might be a real problem. Ultimately, she was left with the impression that Stella was in denial about an ever increasing family issue.

She'd told Jo she knew Maureen was really forgetful, but it surely wasn't Alzheimer's. Really, she just thought Maureen didn't want to come and visit anymore. 'It's too unsettling for her now to think about comin'g up here to stay', she'd said. And that for Stella, was the end of that.

So, back to the question at hand: to teach or not to teach?

In the end, Jo decided to simply not decide.

I've got til Friday to let them know. I'll wait a few more days. I hope I'll have a clearer path after I mull it over a little longer.

It was Wednesday. Her summer break had given her time to take on more of the responsibility with her mom, and that meant a trip to the grocery, at least once a week. This week, it was a Wednesday trip. She picked up the phone to call Maureen.

"Hey Mom. Just calling to make sure you'll be ready around one for grocery shopping."

"Yes, sweetheart. I'll be ready. Have you heard anything from that test we took in Little Rock? I don't think they're gonna find anything, Jo. They're takin' too long to call us back."

"No, I haven't. But tests like this take time. I'm sure we'll receive an answer in a day or two. Let's be patient. I'll see you in a little while. I need to get around and get myself together, clean up here, then I'll be on over."

As she hung up the phone, she made a note to herself on the calendar: 'TALK TO GEORGE AND MAGGIE ABOUT TRIP.'

The rest of the morning and afternoon sped by. She cleaned up her house and made a trip to the grocery with Maureen. She then helped her put away groceries and returned home to take care of her own.

It was after 7 when Jo glanced at the clock.

She was ready for exciting conversation, and George and Maggie could always be counted on for that.

She dialed George's number.

"Hello, my friend. How's everything in God-forsaken-land?" George's familiar voice came through from the other end.

Jo smiled.

"Everything is great over here on the west side of the Mississippi. How about over there in the den-of-iniquity?"

She made no attempt to stifle the mirth in her voice.

"You can't imagine what's happening here. Our cyber division is being inundated with attacks. I've never seen anything like it, Jo. You remember how we used to get only five or six hits a day? Now, we get five or six hits an hour. It's becomin'g impossible to keep everything secure. These guys are getting better. Really sophisticated and really resourceful. I'm not sure what's going on, but something's happening out there in cyberworld."

"How many staffers do you have now? Surely they've increased the number of people you have to monitor and fight these things?"

"Oh, yeah. We're up to 122 people right now. I've never tried to cram so many people into such small spaces. Maggie's doing nothing but setups right now for additional staffers. We're supposed to ramp up to over 200 in the next few months. I'll say one thing, Washington may waste a lot of money, but they're definitely putting their money where their mouth is on this stuff."

"Mmm… well are you two still comin'g for Labor Day? Are you gonna be able to get off?"

"Hell yes, we're comin'g. I haven't taken a decent vacation since you left last year. I gotta have a break, and Maggie's in worse shape than I am. Oh, hey, here she is now. Let me put you on speaker phone and we can all talk."

"Hey, Jo. How ya doin'?"

"Hey, Maggie. I'm good. George was tellin' me how busy ya'll are. You two *are* still comin' for Labor Day, right? I really need quality time with the outside world."

"Oh, yeah. We're comin'. I can't wait to meet George's mom and dad. From what I've heard, I should fit right in with them – they sound like they might be from Alabama, ya know?"

Maggie's laughter rang loud and clear.

"George, you're goin' to risk introducing your parents to another Washington enemy of the Max-and-Maxine rebellion?"

George responded somewhat sheepishly, "I don't think I have a choice. As soon as you told Maggie you'd met them and shared the conversation, she was hooked. Neither one of us could stop her now."

Jo heard Maggie's laughter once again.

"Jo, I don't think those two could throw anything at this redneck gal that she can't deal with. But we'll see… we'll see in a few weeks. Are you goin' with us to see them?"

"Oh, yes. Gina and I are both goin'. Max made sure of that the last time we were there. We had to promise to come. This should be one helluva family reunion, so to speak."

They talked on for another hour. George asking about her mom, revisiting the cyber problems they were encountering. Jo sharing with them her doubts about teaching in the upcomin'g fall classes.

"Well, why are you even worried about it? It's not like you really need the money. I thought you wanted to teach to keep from being so bored out there in never-land. Why don't you just skip a year? It sounds like you've got your hands full with your Mom right now."

"Yeah, you're right, Maggie. But I hate to give it up. I really have enjoyed this last year of teaching. I never thought I would get so much out of it, but I really enjoy interacting with the students. Some of them are really bright, insightful people. We have some really intelligent young people entering this field. The next few years, we shouldn't be short on educated people entering the field of cybersecurity."

"When do you have to let them know for sure?" George asked.

"I've got til August 5th. That's Friday."

"Why don't you sit this one out, Jo? If it continues to evolve as quickly in the next few months as it has in the last three, I'm gonna need your help. I mean, really need some help. Even if you have to do it long distance."

"George, you sound really serious. It's that bad?"

"Yeah, it's that bad. I just have this suspicion... we're headed for something big. Real trouble. There's too much activity. Too many attempts to hack us. In my opinion, this is only the beginning. Only the beginning."

"Ok, well let me think about all this. You guys, I've got to go. Tomorrow will be busy, and I don't need to spend half the night talkin' to you two. I can't wait to actually see you. I'm so lookin' forward to Labor Day."

"Us too, Jo. You take care. We'll talk to you next week."

The fact that Maggie said "us too" wasn't lost on Jo.

I know they're becomin'g a couple. It's just so hard to envision those two together. Surely they'll be ready to share by the time they come to visit. Otherwise, I'll have to force them into a conversation.

She smiled to herself.

Good friends, those two.

As Thursday came calling, Jo was looking forward to the usual coffee break with Gina at the Krusty Kupp. It had almost become a ritual for them.

The phone rang at 8.

"Jo, you comin' this morning?"

"Of course I'm comin'. I'm almost ready. I'll be there by nine, or a few minutes after. If you get there first, order me some scrambled eggs and bacon. Oh, and a large coffee. I'm rather slow this mornin'."

"Ok, see ya in a bit."

Jo was gonna be late.

Damn it, why can't I get it together this mornin'? I need to call Mom. I'll run by after I see Gina. I need to go by and call the doctor's office anyway. I really think we should've already gotten those results.

As she pulled out of the drive, she rolled down all the windows on the jeep.

Gosh, it's a beautiful morning. Thank you, Lord, for another beautiful mountain day.

She plugged her phone into the auxiliary hookup in the jeep. Jo had been astonished to learn she could download music to her phone; but once she figured it out, she rarely ever listened to the radio anymore.

Gotta love ITunes!

She covered the few short miles to town listening to one of her favorites: Bob Seger, Roll Me Away. She thought of Lucy.

I must admit her camper is pretty cool. You know, you have to admire someone like Lucy, she's not afraid to be her own person. No matter how strange some might think that is. I'll spend more time with her when we go back Labor Day. I would like to know more about her life.

The diner came into sight, and sure enough Gina was already there.

So were Jo's scrambled eggs and bacon.

"It's about time. It's almost 9:30. Why are you so late?"

"I just couldn't seem to get my shit together this morning. I don't know where the time went. I did the same things I always do, but today it seemed to take forever."

"Yeah, I have days like that. But not this morning. Isn't it a beautiful day, Jo? I rolled my windows down and soaked up the mountain morning air."

"Me too. I noticed it on the way into town. You know, Gina, I really feel pretty good about things. Everything's comin' together finally. Life doesn't seem so out of sorts. I talked to George and Maggie last night, and I'm so lookin' forward to their visit. Hell, I'm even lookin' forward to seein' Max and Maxine. Can you believe it?"

Gina laughed, a laugh that came from down deep inside.

"I knew you were still there – the girl I once knew is alive and well. Let me make the announcement to the diner!"

Jo hissed. "Don't you dare make a scene in here!"

She was smiling as she spoke through clenched teeth.

"Not today. Today is too perfect for you to mess it up. You just eat your breakfast, Gina Phillips."

They chatted about their plans for Labor Day weekend and Jo's doubts about teaching for the fall semester.

"Oh gosh, it's almost 10:30. I really need to go and check on Mom.

I didn't call this morning 'cause I was runnin' so late. I'm gonna call Dr. Willenfield this mornin' too. I thought we would have the results by now, it's been almost two weeks."

"Yeah, I thought you would have them by now, too. Well go on and let me know if you find out anything from the doc. I gotta spend some time at the center today anyway. There's a girl there I've been working with for several years and she's having some problems. It's always problems, problems."

They shared a smile and knowing look.

"It never ends does it? I really thought by now life would be much simpler. Instead, it's gotten more complicated."

"I don't think it gets simpler until you're just too damn old to care and too crazy to know any difference."

There was real laughter between them at the thought, and the coffee break, also known as their personal therapy session, was over.

Jo and Gina said their goodbyes in the parking lot and went their separate ways.

Gina watched her friend drive away.

What a great morning. What a great friend. Seems like so many of our issues at the beginning of the summer have managed to reconcile themselves. See? Sometimes you just gotta be patient and wait. Isn't that what Mom always said? Anything worth having is worth waiting for.

Jo left the parking lot at the diner once again admiring the beauty of the mountain morning and listening to her favorite songs. Everything about her world seemed to be in perfect harmony.

The one thing, in fact the *only* thing at the moment that marred her perfection was the issue with her mom.

We'll see what the doc has to say. These last few weeks haven't been that bad. Mom's not been so forgetful, and I've had plenty of time to see about both of us. This will work out, too.

She turned down the driveway, and once again realized she needed to find someone to help her clean up around the old home place.

This really needs some attention. I'll ask Melvin if he knows anyone that can help me straighten things up. There's only just a few light repairs that the house needs, the yard needs the most work.

She pulled up and parked beside her Mom's old car.

I'm gonna have to do something about that car, too. She doesn't need to drive. Really, she hasn't driven it anywhere most of the summer. That's another something to see about.

As she hopped out of the jeep, she noticed the front door was open.

That's strange. I bet she came outside to sit on the porch this morning and forgot to close it.

"Mom! Mom!" Jo called out as she went through the front door. No answer.

"Momma! Momma! Are you upstairs?" This time her tone was sharper as she bounded up the stairs.

I should've called this morning. Dammit.

Jo searched the house over, and still no Maureen. By now panic was beginning to take hold of Jo's emotions.

Where can she be? Did she go outside somewhere?

Frantically Jo flew out the front door, searching for any sign of her mom. There just weren't too many places she could be. She wasn't in the garage. She wasn't in the little shed out back. It was like she had vanished.

Calm down, Jo. People don't just disappear off the face of the earth. She's gotta be here somewhere.

For the next several minutes, but what seemed like an eternity to Jo, she called repeatedly for Maureen. So loudly she was sure the neighbors two miles down the road would hear and think she'd lost her mind.

She searched the woods where she often went to escape, calling for Maureen incessantly as she searched.

Finally, an exhausted and hoarse Jo returned to the front porch. Panic and fear were really beginning to take hold of her emotions.

Dear God, what if something's happened to her? I will never forgive myself. I should've insisted on stayin'; Lord, I should've called this morning. Where can she be? What could've happened?

She searched the house and the yard once more, hoping that by some miracle she had missed something, or her mom simply hadn't heard her calling. Desperation tends to blur our sense of reality and common sense, and Jo was in the midst of a desperate situation.

For once in her life, she was simply paralyzed with fear.

Finally, she reached for her phone.

I've got to have some help. I don't know what to do.

She punched "GINA" on her favorites list and waited for it to ring, surely Gina would know what she needed to do next.

"Gina," an almost hysterical Jo spat into the phone. "I can't find Mom… she's not anywhere… I've looked everywhere. In the house, behind the house, in the shed, in the woods. I can't find her! What do I do? What can I do? I don't know what else to do!" At that point Jo was almost in tears. The fear in her voice forced Gina to drop the paper she'd been compiling at the center and focus only on her friends desperate plea.

"Jo, what'd you mean you can't find her? Are you at her house now? Is her car there? Have you called any of her friends to see if they came by to pick her up? What about Stella? Have you talked to her? CALM DOWN. You gotta calm down and think."

"Oh, goodness! I never even thought about Stella. She may have come and got Mom to take her shopping or to the grocery. No, wait. We went to the grocery yesterday. They might be shopping. Let me try to call Stella. I'll call you back."

Jo hung up and immediately tried Stella's cell phone. No answer.

"Shit. Let me try the house. Dear God, I hope she don't answer that one."

Jo was talking aloud to no one but herself. But then panic and fear will make you almost insane.

She dialed the home phone. One ring, two rings, three rings…

For once, please don't let her answer.

Four rings… five rings… just as Jo was about to hang up and breathe a sigh of relief, Stella answered.

"Hey, why are you callin' today? It's only Thursday. I usually don't hear from you til the weekend."

"Stella, I can't find Mom. She's not with you, is she?"

"Well, no. I told you the last time, I just couldn't come and get her to stay with me anymore. Whatcha mean, you can't find her? Where are you? Have you been over to the house? Are you at her house?"

Stella rambled on.

Jo felt as if she were in a time warp. Everything slowed as Stella talked. Time and Stella's voice were morphing into incoherent pieces. It was if she would explode.

"Jo? Jo? Answer me. What's wrong with you? WHERE ARE YOU AT?"

"I'm at Mom's. I gotta go Stella… gotta find her… gotta get some help…"

Jo ended the call and immediately dialed Gina, again.

"Come over here. She's not with Stella. Nobody's come to get her. The front door was standin' wide open when I got here. I don't know what to do. Please come."

She sank down onto the front steps. A sense of fear and dread overwhelmed Jo.

I don't know what to do... I don't even know who to call. Who helps you find lost people? What if she's not lost? What if one of the grandkids came by to see her and took her to town? Surely Stella would know. Surely Mom would've called. She knew I was comin'g over.

Jo's thoughts ran rampant in a nonsensical, jumbled ramble. She didn't hear Gina's car until she stopped beside Jo's jeep.

"Gina, I've never been so scared. I have no idea where she could be... or how to find her. I thought about the grandkids, but surely Stella would've known... what am I gonna do? How am I gonna find her?"

"Give me your phone and sit down."

Gina dialed Stella once again.

"Stella, this is Gina. Did Austin drive down here to see his Grandma?"

"No, Gina. He's at work. I don't have a clue what she could be doin'. The only other person that still drives that might've come and got her would be Mrs. Gray; but Gina, she's been in the hospital. Mom told me that when she was up here visitin'. You don't suppose she's wandered off at home like she did at the mall? I mean, if she really does have that Alzheimer's stuff, she might've wandered off and can't find her way back."

"You need to wind up whatever you're doin' and come on down here. I can take one look at Jo and tell you she doesn't have a clue either and has looked this place over. I'm callin' the sheriff. You need to be on your way NOW, Stella."

Without even giving Stella a chance to respond, Gina hung up the phone and dialed 911.

Gina had been involved in drug rehab for so long, and had dealt with so many multiple arrest victims, she knew most of the police force by first name.

After only two rings, the 911 dispatcher answered the phone.

"911, what is your emergency?" The voice on the other end asked.

"Robbin, this is Gina. Can you patch me through to the Sheriff? I've got a situation, and I'm not sure how to handle it."

"Hey, Gina. Sure, give me a sec."

In only a matter of seconds Robbin had patched her through to Newton County sheriff, John Cole.

"Sheriff." The voice on the other end declared.

"John, this is Gina Phillips. I've got something goin' on and I'm not really sure what to do. I need your help."

Gina spent the next several minutes explaining to the Sheriff what had happened and asking what options they had.

When she hung up the phone, she finally noticed how distraught and tear-stained Jo's face was, and how she was shaking.

She's almost in shock.

"Jo, the sheriff's on his way. Just calm down. We'll find her. She's most likely only wandered off. Now, start from the beginning and tell me what happened."

While Jo relayed the events of the last couple of hours, Gina's mind began to tick off the likely and unlikely possibilities. Where might Miss Maureen be? Her conclusions weren't good.

"Ok, so she hadn't planned to go anywhere, none of the grandkids came and got her. Stella said Mrs. Gray was the only one of her friend's that was still drivin' and she'd been in the hospital. Does your Mom have Mrs. Gray's number written down anywhere, Jo? Does she have the numbers by the phone inside? C'mon, let's go look."

It only took a minute to locate the number they needed, and it was Gina that made the short call to Mrs. Gray.

As she hung up, she turned to face Jo.

"No, no luck. Mrs. Gray's at home, but she's still under the weather from a round of pneumonia. Miss Maureen's not with her."

It was only a few more minutes before they heard the Sheriff in the driveway.

"Ok, now we'll get somewhere. John will know exactly what we need to do. C'mon, Jo."

They met the Sheriff at the front door.

"John, thanks so much for comin' so quick. Jo's in a panic, and to tell you the truth, I'm about to get there myself. We checked with all the family, and the only friend she has that still drives. No one's seen her, talked to her this mornin', or come by to get her. Jo took her to the doctor in Little Rock a few weeks ago because we're afraid she's developed Alzheimer's. She disappeared a few weeks ago with Stella, Jo's sister, on a visit during the holiday. But Jo says she's been much better since comin' back home. What can we do?"

Jo hadn't said a word, but as soon as Gina finished with her statements, she looked at the Sheriff.

"She's wandered off, hasn't she? She's wandered off in these woods. We may not find her for days. How are we gonna find her out here? I've called and called, but she hasn't answered me."

"Now, hang on Jo. Normally we don't accept a missing person's report until they've been missing for 24 hours, however, this is a little different. Given your Mom's recent health and mental issues, we need to start lookin' now. Let me make a call and get Search and Rescue out here. They'll find her. Don't worry, they're trained to find people, no matter what the conditions. And this is not bad terrain. Just be patient. Let me get'em out here. Let's not look for the worst, not yet."

He turned to go to his car, and Gina finally sat down with Jo on the front porch.

"Hang on, Jo and calm down. Let's give these folks a chance to find her, before we think about the worst. Besides, as old as Miss Maureen is, she's probably not too far from the house. They'll find her."

She attempted a weak, but encouraging smile. She got no such response from Jo. Only a fresh round of tears.

Four long and agonizing days later, Search and Rescue found Miss Maureen's body.

She was only two miles from her house, in a ravine. The searchers best guess was that she had fallen; whether she was cognizant of that fact, or unconscious from the fall, they couldn't say.

The house had been full of family, friends, and even complete strangers that had come to help in the search when they brought Jo and Stella the news.

She looked at Gina.

"It's all my fault. I should've called. I should've stayed with her when she came home from Stella's. I could've stopped this."

Jo felt as if she'd suffered a physical blow. For the next several hours it seemed as if her world was crumbling and time stood still.

As the next few days came and went, funeral arrangements were made and family notified. Gina realized what it was like on the outside to witness a grieving person fall apart. She knew this was her all those years ago when Robert had died. She also knew she could do nothing to ease her pain. Not right now, anyway.

For Jo, it was a brand new range of emotions. She hadn't fallen apart so much when her Dad died, but that was a different time, and a different Jo. She'd still had her Mom to turn to, to comfort and to seek comfort from. This time was different. She had moved back to Polk Ridge to take care of her Mom. That was her purpose in life at the moment. And she had failed miserably. Failed to see about Miss Maureen, to keep her safe. Never had she felt so alone, so lost, or so defeated.

The funeral came and went. For Jo, it was one big blur. Gina had called the local doctor for her, and he'd come out to prescribe something to help her through the funeral. Whatever he'd given her, it served to dull the pain and blur the events. It certainly did nothing to alleviate the hollowness in her heart.

The only thing she remembered vividly and clearly, was her conversation with her nephew, Austin.

Everyone had returned to Miss Maureen's house after the funeral for lunch and to have a place to gather and figure out where to go from here. Gina had fixed Jo a plate and set her in the living room.

"You've got to eat something, Jo. I can't remember how many days it's been since I saw you eat anything. Eat now! If for no other reason than because I asked you too."

Jo, still numb and somewhat drugged from the events of the last two days, did as she was told.

She sat. She tried to eat. It was like swallowing cardboard.

The next thing she saw was Austin. He came to sit beside her.

"Aunt Jo, I wanted to ask you something if you don't mind."

Jo pulled herself to as much reality as she could muster. She did really love and admire these boys. She might not know them that well, but she loved them. They were family, her family.

"Alright, sweetheart. What do you want to ask? I don't know if I'll have the answer, but I'll try. You boys look so grown and handsome. Grandma was so proud of you, and I am too."

"Thanks, I was wondering if you would mind if we come to see you now, since Grandma's gone. We usually came down to see her about once a month. Now that I have my driver's license I thought perhaps you wouldn't mind a visit from us? It gives Mom and Dad a break, and we always enjoy comin'. It's so different from home... so peaceful... really different. We wouldn't be much trouble, and we wouldn't have to stay long. We just wondered...

He voice trailed off when Jo didn't immediately respond.

"Oh yes, son. Yes! I'd love for you boys to come and visit. I'm sorry I was so slow to answer. I just wasn't prepared for such a question. You don't have to ask to come see me, you're welcome any time."

As Jo finished her sentence, she was struck by the almost pleading look on Austin's face.

Lord I can't imagine what it must be like to live with Stella Felsenthal. Bless his heart. I should really spend more time with them. I should know my nephews better than I do.

"Thanks, Aunt Jo. This might not be the best time, but we'd really like to get to know the only Aunt we've got. Especially since you're back and so close now."

He gave her a quick hug and then was gone. For Jo it was a turning point. The numbness and fog began to lift. It wasn't gone, but it began to lift.

Life continues on. Although the seasons may change, life is continuous. New relationships replace old ones. And sometimes, old relationships become new again. Either way, life goes on.

CHAPTER 17

All alone at the end of the evening...
When the bright lights have faded to blue...
When there's nothing to believe in...
Take it to the limit
Take it to the limit
Take it to the limit, one more time.

Eagles

WEDNESDAY, AUGUST 29TH, 2012 dawned, and Jo was acutely aware of a change in the smell of the air.

Fall is comin'g to the Ozarks. Fall is comin'g and I have very little family left to finish this journey with. And now the very reason I came here is gone.

The last several weeks Jo had spent in near seclusion. The only person she'd spent any time with was Gina.

She'd taken a few short phone calls from George and Maggie and none of the five calls from Paul.

The pain was too deep and too fresh for idle chit chat. She needed time. Time to think, to heal, to remember, and someone to share it with that really understood.

For Jo, that time was spent at home alone. Gina was the only person she turned to in those first weeks. To share the guilt and remorse;

the memories and pain. She was the only one left that remembered all the fun times with Miss Maureen and Tom. She was the only one that could truly understand her sense of loss. And in many ways, Gina was the only one that understood her burden of guilt.

Her phone rang and pulled her from her thoughts. It was Gina. "Hey. Whatcha' doin'?"

"Sittin' on the back porch smellin' the air. What are you doin'?"

"Smellin' the air? Seriously, Jo. That's what it's come down to? You just gonna sit there and smell the air for another month or so?"

"No. Yes. I mean, I don't know. I don't wanna do anything else."

"Well, put on some clothes. I'm comin' over there. We're goin' for a ride."

"A ride? I don't wanna go for a stupid ride. What are you thinkin'? It's only eight o'clock in the mornin'. We don't have anywhere to go."

"Yes we do. Get dressed."

She hung up before Jo could reply.

Right or wrong be damned. She's wallowed in grief and pity long enough. She'll just have to get mad. Life did not stop with Miss Maureen's death, and it's not good for her to sit up there all alone. Time for a healthy dose of reality.

Gina locked the door as she went out and climbed in the car.

I know where I'm gonna take her. It'll snap her out of this. And besides, I'm tired of fielding calls. If it's not George and Maggie, it's Paul. I haven't talked to Paul Collections in nearly forty years. I don't even know how he got my number. Geez! It's time to move on Jo. I know, I've been there.

As she backed out of the drive, she cranked up the stereo.

A little Elvis will help me deal with this and help Jo snap back to life.

She grinned.

If for no other reason, to simply tell me to turn the old shit off!

As she turned into the drive, she saw Jo standing on the porch.

Well, at least she got dressed.

She pulled up and hollered.

"C'mon, let's go. Daylight's a wastin' Jo."

"Where are we goin'? I told you I don't really wanna go anywhere."

"Yeah, I know that's what you said. But we've got somewhere we need to go. C'mon."

Jo sulked all the way to car.

"You can forget that sulkin' workin' on me today. I've been up here constantly. I've talked to you, sat with you, fed you, listened to you, felt sorry for you. I've done everything a good friend would do, everything except for this. So now you can smile or frown, but we're takin' a ride."

Gina reached to turn the stereo up again.

"Elvis? Really Gina? That's what we're gonna listen to?"

"Yep. Unless you have a better idea."

"Well, I do. Here, let me play my phone. At least there's something besides Elvis on my playlist."

Gina smiled.

There you go. Go ahead and come back to life.

Gina rolled the windows down and headed for the old iron bridge. It had been years since she'd been there, but she knew from all the young people she'd counselled that it was still a hangout.

She flashed a smile at Jo.

"You'll like where we're goin', trust me."

"Famous last words, right?"

Gina began to sing with the radio. She turned to look at Jo and mouthed 'sing'.

Finally, Jo joined in. The Eagles were playing one of their favorites, *Take It To The Limit.*

As the song ended, Jo recognized where they were, and figured out where they were going.

"The Old Iron Bridge. That's where you're takin' me."

"Yes ma'm, yes I am. We had some good times there, Jo. If you're gonna wallow in pity and guilt, we're gonna at least go somewhere that brings back good memories. I came up here after Robert died. I really don't know how many times I came; it helped me seem close to him and closer to the memories we made up here on Friday nights and weekends. Back when we owned the world. Back when everything seemed right and good and… free. Isn't that what you're lookin' for? A way to feel right with world again? A way to seem like there's something to live for and look forward to?"

Jo looked as if she was about to cry.

"No, no! No you don't. You've cried your heart out these last few weeks. And if you're not finished, that's fine. But you're not gonna cry here. Here, you're gonna look for a way to heal, to move on, to find happiness again."

"Oh, Gina. It's not that I don't think I'll be happy again; it's that I feel so lost. So guilty. The whole reason I came home was to see about Mom. Now, it's like I haven't accomplished anything. I gave up my work and my life in Washington to move home and take care of her. Now, it all seems so pointless. So wasted. I failed."

Gina just stared.

"Jo, what about I'm about to say is gonna seem hard. It's probably gonna make you mad, but I wouldn't be your friend if I didn't say it."

"You need to crawl out of your 'me, me, me' thoughts and look at the last year from a different point of view. Miss Maureen needed you. Maybe the time she needed you was shorter than you thought it was gonna be, but nonetheless, you came home and brightened an old woman's world. For goodness sake, she was in her eighties. You know what I would have given to have my Mom till she was in her eighties? You know what a blessin' it is to have eighty years to live life? You don't control how long someone has here on this earth. All you can do is spend time with them while they're here. You did that. You were here when she needed you the most."

"No, I failed her when she needed me most."

"No you didn't. Her death was between her and God. You weren't ever a part of that equation, like it or not. We like to think we can control everything, but you, or me, or no one else has any say in that event."

"And for the record, your time here hasn't been wasted. You've become *my* best friend again. We've shared more in the last few months than we did in all those years of high school. I've confided in you, I've fought with you, and I've learned more about myself thanks to you. I wouldn't call that wasted time."

"And one more thing, it was time for you to come home. The military isn't the only life you can or should have. You grew up here. You still have family around here. You need something besides all that "cyber" shit to fill your life. I can promise you that when *you're* eighty, and lookin' back on life, fightin' cyber nuts won't be what makes you smile."

"You never do know when to shut up do you, Gina? You just yack, yack, yack; on and on."

Gina stopped long enough to contemplate the fact that she might've touched a nerve. But then, maybe that was a good thing. At least some emotion besides grief and tears was hanging out inside there.

Jo turned to Gina. Time to give her friend her full attention.

"But then, that's one of the things I like about you most."

And she graced Gina with one of the most genuine smiles she'd had in weeks. One that reached all the way to those sad, cried-out eyes.

"Are we gonna sit here and you preach to me, or can we get out and walk around? C'mon."

They got out of the car.

Thank God. At least she really smiled. I wasn't sure this was gonna work.

Somehow their walking and their talking took them across the iron bridge. Although ancient and unfit for cars, the old lady had no trouble bearing the weight of anyone who chose to walk across. Old planks creaked and moaned as if to say 'easy, I'm old and cranky; take your time crossing and make sure you pause to enjoy the view'.

Gina stopped.

"Stop right here Jo. Now look down. Take a good look at that reflection. What do you see?"

"I certainly don't see the teenager that used to be up here lookin' down," she said with a laugh.

"No, you don't. You see a grown woman that's lived a great life. You chose your path and you stepped out into a great big world. I'd say you've had a pretty good run with it and now you're at a crossroads. If there's anything that you regret, if there's anything that you haven't done you wanted to do, here's your chance. Quit wallowing in the pity over 'woulda, coulda, shoulda'."

"Hell, Jo, you're in the prime of your life. You have experienced a loss, and grievin' over that is normal. But it's not normal to sit and brood thinkin' it's your fault, or that you had any control over what happened with Miss Maureen. Find a way to be happy with the memories you have and get on with life."

Her tone had softened when she spoke again.

"It's not easy. I remember losing Robert like it was yesterday. But life for those of us that remain must go on."

"I know, Gina. I understand all the logical, common sense answers to these questions. It's just really hard to be logical when your heart is involved."

"You're right. It is really hard. But sometimes you gotta give yourself a swift kick in the ass and make yourself listen to the logic. Time for that swift kick, Jo. And I know exactly what that's gonna be."

Oh, dear God… what?"

"You're gonna call George and Maggie and tell them you are sorry you've been ignoring them. Tell them that you're still expectin' Labor Day company on Saturday. And then, you're gonna call Paul Collections cause I'm damn tired of takin' *his* calls, too. Got it?"

"No. Gina I'm nowhere near ready for company. It's Wednesday. The house is in shambles. I've not bought not the first thing to get ready for company. No."

"Oh, yeah. You're gonna call'em. 'Cause I already told them you were still expectin' them, and that you would call them tonight just like you've done for the last six months. I suggest we get busy and whip that house into shape. We've only got two days."

"You gotta be kiddin' me? Why did you tell them that? You straight out lied. I told you I was gonna tell them not to come, just to go straight to his mom and dad's."

"Yeah, that's what you told me, but you didn't tell *them*. So I figured you just needed a good push. And anyway, a little white lie never hurt anybody. Come Saturday, you'll be glad I did it. Now, Jo Felsenthal, let's go clean up a house."

"I really don't like it when you do shit I don't know about, Gina. It never fails to get crazier than I ever thought it could when I put you in charge."

She did know one thing for sure and certain though. The best friend she had in Gina Ingram might be gone, but she'd certainly discovered a new one in Gina Phillips.

As for Gina, she'd never really had any doubts about Jo Felsenthal; she knew enough about life to know she'd been right. *Just leave it alone, it'll sort itself out.*

Their lives had crossed paths all those years ago for a reason.

Everyone needs a best friend.

Sunday, September 2nd, 2012

The jeep was loaded, and Gina was on her way.

George and Maggie had already left for God only knows what kind of visit with Max and Maxine.

One thing was for sure, this would be a holiday for the record books. She couldn't wait to see Maggie with Max. She couldn't wait to see how George *introduced* Maggie to Max. After the last couple of days, she knew damn well it wouldn't be as his 'co-worker'.

She wasn't sure she was up to a debate with Max, but thanks to Gina, she wasn't sure she wasn't ready either.

So much of what I worried about with Gina has managed to work itself out. So many of those questions just needed a little time and an open mind to be answered. A catastrophic life event didn't hurt either.

She stopped for a second to gaze at the beauty that surrounded her. Mom always loved the flowers and the mountains that surrounded us when I was growing up.

I'll miss you so much, Mom. But I'm so glad we had some time together before you had to go. At least I'll have something to smile about, these last few months were great. And because of you, I finally came home.

I've spent a lifetime beyond the Ozarks, maybe now I could spend the rest of my time....

Her cell phone rang.

"Hello, Paul. Listen, I just wanted to apologize...."

AUTHOR AND WRITER, NATALIE R VICE has spent a lifetime preparing for the stories created in *The Scrapbook Series*. A collection of stories focused on the lives of Jo and Gina, two women raised in the Ozark Mountains of northern Arkansas. She draws upon her life experiences as a young woman raised in small town America for the funny and sometimes dysfunctional adventures of the characters as they come together for the pursuit of lost friendship and new adventures.

Born in 1965, on an Air Force Base, her parents returned to the small town way of life to live and raise their 3 children. Natalie has spent most of her life within a 50 mile radius of that same small town, observing and finding humor in the everyday "mishaps" that occur when life is lived in a small town.

She has been an author, blogger and freelance writer for well over a decade and holds a Bachelor of Science in Accounting. In addition to creating *The Scrapbook Series*, she also offers services for the business, finance and education industries.

*In 1977, at the TG&Y in Fayette, Al, I bought a plaque
of an old Irish proverb/prayer. One of those lines reads:*

Take time to dream, it is hitching your wagon to a star.

*I still have the plaque; it hangs on my office wall and
I still take time to dream. In following the dream of
writing, I created the characters of Jorja Felsenthal and
Regina Ingram and began their story.*

THE SCRAPBOOK SERIES IS an opportunity to look at life through the eyes of the most unsung hero in American life: the everyday, average woman. We take life as it comes and find a way to deal with unbelievable situations: we laugh, we cry, we struggle. We get angry and frustrated. We are overjoyed and in tears simultaneously. We love in ways that are sometimes completely insane, and we reach for each other…. we reach for our girl friends. In doing so, we reach for a better tomorrow, while we learn to make the most of today.

To steal a phrase from Jackson Browne's *Everyman*, I wanted to create the "everywoman" in Jo and Gina. I wanted my readers to be able to identify with their life experiences. To read about one of their predicaments and say "Ah, yes. Been there done that."

I needed to be able to write about things, events and people that I was comfortable with. In my writings, although none of these characters are real, they were created from many of my own life experiences, interactions, thoughts, and beliefs. I needed to write in ways that provided a connection between myself, my work, and my readers.

I am a woman, so I wrote about women.

I have lived life and made mistakes, made the best of it and moved on. So have Jo and Gina.

As I wrote about their low moments, I cried. As I wrote about their funny escapades, I laughed. I want my readers to feel those same emotions. I want them to walk away from the story of Jo and Gina empowered as a woman, with hope in their heart and joy for tomorrow!

Below, I've included the Old Irish Proverb in its entirety. I hope it brings all of you as much inspiration as it always has to me.

> *Take time to work, it is the price of success.*
>
> *Take time to think, it is the source of power.*
>
> *Take time to play, it is the secret to perpetual youth.*
>
> *Take time to read, it is the foundation of wisdom.*
>
> *Take time to be friendly, it is the road to happiness.*
>
> *Take time to dream, it is hitching your wagon to a star.*
>
> *Take time to love and to be loved, it is the privilege of the gods.*
>
> *Take time to look around, the day is too short to be selfish.*
>
> *Take time to laugh, it is the music of the soul.*

Women of the Ozarks,
Scrapbook Series…

Book X, A Prequel

NATALIE R. VICE

Can friendship last a lifetime?

Everyone says that hindsight is 20/20. If that's true, how much of that image in the rear view affects who we are today, or who we will become tomorrow?

Jo Felsenthal and Gina Ingram were the closest of childhood friends back in Polk Ridge, Arkansas. Growing up in this beautiful, close-knit Ozark community, they were surrounded by love and laughter.

But as these girls grew into women, choices were made, and life took them in very different directions.

Now, they're just hours away from a reunion several decades in the making. A out-of-the-blue Facebook "friend" request has snowballed into a face-to-face meeting. Both women are dealing with mixed emotions—excitement, nostalgia, and more than a little apprehension.

In *Memories of Tomorrow*, Jo and Gina weave their way through childhood memories and difficult life choices. They ponder how to cross over all their yesterdays to the girls they once were. Can they find anything in common after so many years spent living such different lives?

If you like The Sometimes Sister and Hurricane Season, you'll love the *Women of the Ozarks Scrapbook Series*.

Book One

Two separate paths. One enduring friendship.

Jo Felsenthal and Gina Ingram were girls of the '60s and '70s and grew into young women during one of the most turbulent social times in American history. The cultural forces of those tumultuous times had a tremendous impact on the choices they made and the women they became. As these two women, now in their fifth decade of life, look back to see just how far they've come, they long for the friendship they once shared.

Having traveled the world for nearly forty years as a military officer and NSA liaison, Jo Felsenthal is now forced to take a step backward and return to her childhood home of Polk Ridge, Arkansas. Stepping back into this old (and mostly forgotten) territory comes with its challenges. Her mom's health is failing, her career and personal life are in freefall, and she hasn't connected with anyone in Polk Ridge in a lifetime.

Gina Phillips has spent a lifetime facing more adversity than she cares to recall. From teenage mom, to widow, to social worker, she has made her way and her life in Polk Ridge, one of the poorest towns in one of the poorest counties in Arkansas. So when Gina decides unwind on her back porch after work, she's more than surprised when a familiar, yet long neglected friend pops up in her Facebook feed. Yet there she is: Jo! Gina's dearest childhood friend—now a complete stranger—is back in town. Her quick click on "friend request" is about to have lasting consequences….

Can these women find a way to bridge a lifetime of separation and recapture the friendship of their youth? They'll soon find out if a bucket full of childhood memories is enough to reignite a once-treasured friendship long abandoned. Set in a beautiful, close-knit Ozark community, *Tomorrow's Promise* is a story of family and friendship. Through joy and despair, Jo and Gina will walk you down a nostalgic road and perhaps into a promising future. If you like The Book Club and The Summer Girls, you'll love the *Women of the Ozarks Scrapbook Series.*

How Much of Your Future Depends on Your Past?

After decades apart, childhood friends Jo Felsenthal and Gina Ingram spend their first summer together after more than forty years. A few weeks spent revisiting life as the girls they used to be and getting to know each other as the women they've become has shown them that time and circumstances have changed them both.

They're different women with different ideals and different convictions. Gina has spent her life in their hometown of Polk Ridge, Arkansas, nestled in the Ozark mountains as a counselor for the poor and drug addicted. She's sympathetic and open minded to others' hardships. Jo, by contrast, has lived her life in the military—an environment with a single-minded purpose and a demand for rigid discipline.

For Jo, blending back into a community that distrusts the very government she has spent her life defending, leaves her completely at odds with the people Gina seems to adore. When Jo meets Gina's friends Max and Maxine, she's thrown for a loop as these two conspiracy driven hippies challenge her beliefs about the government and law—all of which has shaped her into the woman she is today. Her instant dislike of Gina's friends suddenly threatens the newly reunited childhood friends.

In *Crossing Yesterday*, the second book in the *Women of the Ozarks Scrapbook Series*, Jo and Gina are forced to ask: Just how far apart can two people be and still find common ground?

If you like Beach House for Rent and The Book of Lost Friends, you'll love the *Women of the Ozarks Scrapbook Series*.

Book Three

It's the stuff you *don't* see coming, that changes your life's path.

Throughout your life you learn to plan, prepare, and plan some more. You learn to cope with the expected. It's the stuff you don't see coming that can be your undoing. Jo Felsenthal and Gina Ingram's lives are no different.

When Gina's son has a child out of wedlock and she learns that her deceased husband also fathered an illegitimate child, her carefully constructed family life is turned inside out. Gina's longtime friend and sometime boyfriend Melvin, suddenly seems completely uninterested in her latest turn of events. If she has ever needed a friend, it's now.

Jo has her own set of issues. She's confronted with revisiting her feelings for Paul Collections, the high school sweetheart she couldn't make room for all those years ago. Jo also finds herself confronted with a sister that seems to be in the midst of a mid-life crisis and co-workers in the midst of a blossoming romance.

In the *Unraveling*, life's plans seem to be quickly dissolving. They had a path they wanted to follow. They were making careful preparations for that path. Now, it seems that everyone and everything is conspiring to turn the most carefully constructed plans upside down! How did it all get so complicated?

Suddenly, finding a lost friendship seems like the easiest part of their lives.

If you like Before We Were Yours and The Sisters Café, you'll love the *Women of the Ozarks Scrapbook Series*.

Book Four

Recapturing love and a sense of adventure isn't as freeing as you would think…

Ready to take advantage of retirement, lifelong friends Jo Felsenthal and Gina Ingram plan a two-week trip to sunny California. In this new environment, far from home, the two women finally feel free to say and do what they want. Gina finds she's rather fond of pot and Jo re-discovers her love of wine. They finally understand the phrase, *California dreamin'.*

What was supposed to be a short trip, turns into months away from their home in the Ozarks. Gina begins to feel the increasing tug of her responsibilities at home in Polk Ridge, but is reluctant to leave her never-ending vacation in the Golden State.

Jo, on the other hand, has finally come to the staggering

revelation that she's once again fallen in love with teen sweetheart Paul Collections. This time, though, Paul isn't necessarily a free man.

As realities in their hometown of Polk Ridge, Arkansas keep calling, Jo and Gina find themselves trying to answer an age old question: Is the grass really any greener on the other side?

If you like The Sometimes Sister and Beach House for Rent, you'll love the *Women of the Ozarks Scrapbook Series*.

Book Five

The Fates giveth, and the Fates taketh away…

Almost a decade has passed since a fateful Facebook friend request brought childhood friends Jo Felsenthal and Gina Ingram back together after a life apart. The inseparable girls of '76 are now older, wiser, and best friends again. They've shared tears and laughter, anger and happiness, trials and triumphs. They have stopped searching for the girls they used to be and found lasting friendship in the women they have become.

Jo has rekindled a once-lost love and Gina has reconciled herself with life in the Ozarks. The girl who once had no idea which path to choose, has found that the path has chosen her. The mountains, the people, and the family Gina has fought so hard to hold together have given her the sweetest gift of all: enduring love.

Jo and Gina's friendship has been tried and tested for almost half a century. Together, they have experienced girlish dreams and desires, love and loss, happiness and regrets. But most importantly they've grown into women who cherish a lasting friendship.

Then fate deals their enduring friendship one final blow...

Wait For Me, is the fifth and final book in the Women Of The Ozarks Scrapbook Series, and will share the poignant final stories of two women who have seen so much and found friendship through it all.